ENTWINED FATES

THE INFINITE CITY

TIFFANY ROBERTS

ENTWINED FATES

He met his destined mate too soon.

Bold, kind, and adventurous, Kiara was everything Volcair needed in his stiff, formal life. Along with his pet inux, Cypher, the three were inseparable during Volcair's years on Earth. But the same winds of fate that brought them together as children tore them apart again. With half a universe separating them, years sped by, and Kiara seemed lost to him forever. Angry and bitter, he threw himself into military service for the Entris Dominion, seeking escape from the pain of loss.

When chance brings them together again nearly two decades later, Volcair finds that his feelings for Kiara have only grown— he needs her. Have they been granted a second chance, or has time opened a rift between them that cannot be crossed?

To those who believe in love and second chances.

ONE

London, Capital of the United Terran Federation, Earth
Terran Year 2075

VOLCAIR FOLDED his arms across his abdomen and looked down at the floor. This was his last chance, his final opportunity to make an escape. He was doomed if this didn't work.

"I do not feel well, Father," he said, hunching forward for added effect.

Cypher turned his four yellow optics up toward Volcair. The creature was an inux, a robotic companion of sorts, and currently resembled a zeget—a long-bodied, four-legged creature with a featherlike crest along its head and a short, stubby tail. Zegets were native to Volcair's homeworld, Korous, which he'd not seen for years.

Tilting his head, Cypher produced a series of concerned warbles and clicks. His silvery metal scales rippled as though he were about to change shape.

"Oh?" Ambassador Syntrell Vantricar Caltraxion put his

hands on Volcair's shoulders, turned the boy to face him, and knelt. His long, blue hair, so similar to Volcair's, fell forward to frame his narrow face. "Your stomach, is it, Son?"

Volcair studied his father's faintly glowing *qal*, the markings every volturian was born with. Vantricar's *qal* was like Volcair's in pattern and coloration—flowing blue-white lines and circles that emphasized musculature and bone structure, exemplary of their ancestral *qalar*, the Syntrell. Vantricar's markings were far fuller and more intricate, however, because he had followed the old tradition of having his mate's *qal* added to his own to solidify their mating bond. Volcair could not look upon his father without seeing his mother's markings.

The reminder of his mother, Commander Syntrell Aliari Morenna—dead five years now—produced a sinking feeling in Volcair's belly. If nothing else, it added a touch of truth to his ploy.

He frowned as deeply as he could and nodded.

Vantricar glanced up at the elevator's floor indicator.

Volcair was unfamiliar with most of the terran symbols it displayed; he knew the numerals for the floor upon which he and his father kept their quarters and those for the ground level and the commissary, but everything else was foreign to him. Only two things were certain—their destination was on the building's top floor, and they were nearly there.

Once they arrived at the party, Volcair would be trapped. Vantricar tolerated no interruptions while he was working.

"Strange. You have not mentioned anything before this point," Vantricar said. He gently pressed his hand to Volcair's forehead.

"I did not want to disappoint you, Father." Somehow, Volcair forced the corners of his mouth farther down. "I know this is important to you. I will return to our quarters and rest, so as not to trouble you."

"What a considerate son I have." Vantricar's lips tilted in a smirk. "But I cannot bear to leave you alone, my child. Perhaps there will be a couch at the gathering upon which you may rest."

Volcair's brows fell. "I...I would be more comfortable in our quarters, Father. And I would not be alone. Cypher will accompany me."

Cypher's scaled head feathers perked, and he clicked in agreement.

Vantricar smoothed back Volcair's hair before returning his hand to the boy's shoulder. "You will attend this function alongside me, Volcair Vantricar. Our relations with these terrans are young—younger than you. Our *qalsarn* would like our peoples to be good friends, and to become friends, we must freely explore the things we have in common. *Family* is one of those things."

"But all that is *your* job. *You* are the ambassador, Father, not me. The *qalsarn* did not appoint me to a post."

"Regardless of your position or lack thereof, you have a duty to our people, and I expect you to honor it."

"Mother is *dead* because of duty!" Volcair pulled back, but his father did not release him.

Cypher whimpered and curled around Volcair's leg.

Vantricar's jaw muscles ticked, and he tightened his grip on Volcair's shoulders. "Your mother died protecting our people. There is no greater form of heroism. What I ask of you is a tiny thing compared to that, but it will be of great benefit to our people."

Tears stung Volcair's eyes. He'd only been four years old when his mother was killed in combat, but the pain had never faded. Cypher—who'd been a gift from Aliari when Volcair was only two or three—kept the memory of her close to the surface all the time. Sometimes, that meant joy. Others, it meant pain.

"I would rather have her *here*, with us," Volcair said.

"As would I," Vantricar rasped, "but we have only each other, Volcair, and you must remain with me. Besides, this may not be as boring as you expect. I have been told the terran Minister of Interplanetary Relations has a child close to your age."

Volcair wiped his eyes before any tears could fall and clenched his jaw. He didn't want to attend this gathering; he'd endured a dozen such functions on half a dozen worlds over the last few years, and each had been, at best, tedious. "You always say I will make friends with alien children, but we never stay anywhere long enough for that to happen."

"I think this world will be different," Vantricar said gently. "The nature of my task here is not the same as the other places we have been. Try for me, Son. Give me one hour. If your mood has not changed by then, I will allow you to return to our quarters."

To nine-year-old Volcair, an hour at a boring party was the most torturous experience possible—especially when he was forced to wear this formal Volturian suit with its high collar and snug fit. He'd never understood why ambassadors and diplomats were always interested in meeting each other's families. Volcair had never been asked to contribute to any of the negotiations his father was involved in, so why did he need to memorize the names of foreign government officials and their immediate families? What did it matter whether they knew who he was?

Volcair *was* old enough to know this was important to his father. Vantricar treated his duty to the Entris Dominion as the most important thing in his life—especially since his mate's death.

A tiny thing.

Releasing a shaky, frustrated breath, Volcair nodded. "One hour. No longer."

"Thank you." Smiling, Vantricar released Volcair's shoulders and rose, turning to face the elevator doors.

Moments later, the elevator's gentle hum ceased. The doors slid open with a soft *ding*.

Volcair, with Cypher in tow, followed his father into the hallway. He couldn't help but look upon his surroundings in wonder. The lower portions of the walls were crafted of dark, polished wood with a hint of red. The wood was carved with flowing, intricate patterns that enhanced its strange grain, making it unlike any wood he'd seen.

They stopped at a pair of large doors. Several guards representing the species of the various envoys who'd gathered on Earth—volturian, borian, vorgal, and azhera—stood to either side of the doors, with a pair of terrans on the inside.

The terran and volturian guards turned toward Vantricar and bowed their heads in a display of respect.

"Ambassador Syntrell Vantricar Caltraxion," one of the terrans said, his accent putting a unique spin on the name, "it is our honor to receive you."

Volcair's translator implant granted him understanding of the words spoken in the terran's native language, which his father had called *English*. He'd seen many terrans in the few weeks he'd spent on Earth with his father thus far. They weren't very different from volturians in size, shape, and appearance, though their features were a bit softer. The strangest things about them—apart from their language—were their coloring and lack of *qal*.

Vantricar bowed his head deeply. "It is my honor to be received."

The terrans pulled the doors open. Vantricar, Volcair, and Cypher proceeded into the room beyond.

The space they entered was large and high-ceilinged. The wall straight ahead, along with a portion of the ceiling over it, was comprised almost entirely of glass, offering an open view of the blue sky and the city outside—*London*—stretching toward the distant horizon. Several diverse groups of people were clustered around the tables, engaged in conversations that filled the room with a soft, warm hum. It was strange to have diplomats from so many species meeting at once outside of Arthos, where countless peoples came together, but the terrans were new to the intergalactic community. Vantricar had explained that these people were still forging alliances and establishing their place in the cosmos.

Volcair shifted his focus to the tables, all of which were arranged with a variety of utensils and settings. Each bore a large, circular display at its center, laden with assorted foods from different worlds.

"Father," Volcair said, "they seem to have mixed up the table settings."

Vantricar paused to glance at the nearest table. "*Did* they?"

He often spoke in that tone when he wanted Volcair to look closer and think.

Volcair furrowed his brow. "No?"

"Why?"

"Because...because they want...everyone to sit together?"

Vantricar nodded and turned his attention to a pair of approaching terrans. "Minister Moore, I am honored by your invitation. Thank you for having us."

Volcair studied the terrans. One was male and the other

female, both tall with dark hair and brown skin. He wished he'd denied his father's request and returned to their quarters; he had no problem with these terrans, but the conversations his father had with such officials were boring and always saw Volcair forgotten within a few minutes, regardless of the species involved.

Perhaps he could sneak out and hang around the guards; they usually had more interesting things to say than the diplomats they protected.

As though aware of Volcair's intention to flee, Cypher positioned himself behind the boy's legs and brushed his metal scales over Volcair's pants, cutting off Volcair's only potential escape route.

Volcair glanced down at the inux and muttered, "Traitor."

Cypher's crest feathers twitched, and his lips parted in a grin, displaying his sharp, metallic teeth.

"Ambassador Syntrell Vantricar Caltraxion," Minister Moore said with a smile, spreading his arms wide, "I'm pleased you could join us."

Volcair's father dipped his head. "The pleasure is mine. And let it be Vantricar, shall we?"

Minister Moore bowed his head in return. "Of course! As long as you call me Isaiah." He stepped back and slowly swept his hand to the side, motioning his family forward. "Allow me to introduce my wife, Jada."

Jada lowered her chin with a smile. A few strands of her long, braided hair fell forward. "It's good to finally meet you, Vantricar. Isaiah has told me so many wonderful things about your homeworld. It sounds beautiful."

"Thank you," Vantricar replied. "I have found great beauty here on your Earth, as well. I am glad our people can be friends."

"As am I."

"And this"—Isaiah twisted to reach behind him—"is our daughter, Kiara." Placing a hand on his daughter's back, he urged the little female forward.

The girl stood no taller than Volcair's shoulders. Her soft yellow dress billowed out in layers at the waist, its hem resting atop the toes of her white shoes. The fabric's color complemented her dark skin. Her black hair was smoothed down in front but erupted in a mass of curls at the back of her head, which bounced with each of her little movements.

Kiara kept her hands clasped behind her back and her body angled slightly away from Volcair, but when she lifted her head and smiled, something heated in his chest. Her big, warm brown eyes shone with inner light, and her smile was so bright and confident that it was completely at odds with her demure posture.

The heat in Volcair's chest spread up to his face.

"We are honored to meet you, Kiara," Vantricar said. He placed a hand on Volcair's shoulder and guided him forward. "This is my son, Volcair Vantricar, but just Volcair will do."

Volcair's throat constricted as he stared at Kiara. He'd never experienced anything like what he was feeling; this was something new, wonderful, and mysterious, something exhilarating and terrifying all at once.

Kiara stepped away from her parents to stand directly in front of Volcair. Without hesitation, she reached up and trailed her fingertips over the *qal* on his cheek. "You're so pretty. Like a star."

"Kiara!" Isaiah and Jada said simultaneously.

Volcair's skin tingled at her touch; the sensation coursed along his *qal* in a low, steady thrum. He recoiled—not because it was unpleasant, but because it was unexpected. Because it was *powerful*.

Isaiah grasped Kiara's shoulders and pulled her back. "Please, accept my apologies. My daughter means no offense. She is young and enthusiastic, and often lets her excitement overpower her judgment."

Kiara frowned, tipping her head back to look up at her father.

He bent down until his mouth was next to her ear. "It's rude to run up to someone and touch them, Kiara. Those markings are called *qal*, and they are very important to our guests. *Qal* represent their *qalar*, which is like their clan, or their extended bloodline."

"But they *glowed*, Daddy." Her voice was soft, sweet, and lilting.

Cypher forced his way through Volcair's legs, tilted his head to one side, and raised his crest feathers.

Vantricar gave Volcair's shoulder a gentle squeeze; the bewildered boy knew the gesture was a prompt, but he wasn't sure what his father wanted him to do.

Volcair glanced up to find his father staring at him with a furrowed brow and a small frown. After a few moments of scrutinizing Volcair, Vantricar lifted his eyebrows and tipped his head toward the terrans.

"Um, I..." Volcair pressed his suddenly dry lips together and looked back at Kiara. Seeing her appear so deflated after her father's admonishment made Volcair's heart ache. "There is no need for apologies, Minister Moore. I have taken no, um...no offense."

"We can all learn much from the innocent enthusiasm of our children," said Vantricar, patting his son's back. "The young see past the differences by which we divide ourselves as adults. It is a beautiful thing, is it not?"

"It is," Jada said, smiling at Volcair before turning to brush her fingers down Isaiah's arm. "Why don't we let the children get better acquainted while we introduce Vantricar to the other guests?"

Isaiah straightened and dropped his hands from Kiara's shoulders. "Yes. I'm sure they will enjoy some time away from us adults."

"Behave yourself, Volcair," Vantricar said, "and be polite. You need only endure fifty-five more minutes and you may leave."

Volcair looked at Kiara again; her smile had returned, though it was softer and subtler. "I think I might stay, Father. I am...feeling a little better."

"Oh? I am glad. Seek me out should you change your mind." With a final pat on Volcair's shoulder, Vantricar joined Isaiah and Jada and walked with them to another part of the room.

"Are you sick?" Kiara asked.

Volcair frowned. "No. I mean, yes. Well, I was not feeling very well for a little while, but... It was probably just because of the elevator. Having to travel so far in it likely upset my stomach."

"The lift makes my tummy feel funny, too. I'm glad you're better. How old are you?"

"Uh... Nine, in terran years. That is what my father said, anyway."

"Wow, really? I'm only seven, but I'm very grown-up for my age." She took a step closer and lowered her gaze to Cypher. "I like your pet. What's his name?"

"Cypher. But he is not a pet, he is an inux. More of a...companion."

The only steady companion Volcair had had for the last several years.

Cypher eased forward, stood on his hind legs, and placed his metal front paws on Kiara's belly, extending his neck to peer up at her face.

She gasped and leaned away.

"Do not worry," said Volcair. "He is friendly as long as I am not threatened."

"Is he a robot?"

"Sort of. But he is also a living creature. Inux are...unique."

Cypher made a few clicking and buzzing sounds before nuzzling his snout against Kiara's dress. She giggled. His scales rippled from nose to tail before he dropped back onto all fours and curled his long body around her legs.

"What's he doing?" she asked.

"He likes you."

Her large eyes met Volcair's. "He does?"

Volcair nodded, and his face heated anew. "And...and I think I do, too."

Her smile widened. "I like you, too. We can be mates."

Volcair's mouth went dry, and his heartbeat echoed in his ears. *Mates?* That's what his mother and father had been, but volturians usually didn't take mates until their twenties or thirties. "Um...are we not too young?"

"My mum says you're never too young or too old to make friends," she replied.

A wave of relief eased Volcair's tension, and he released a slow breath as the heat in his face finally faded. His father had told him that his translator wouldn't be exact—terran languages were only newly assimilated to the database, and it always took time to sort out imperfect translations, especially for languages that had many words with similar meanings.

Volcair bowed his head. "I would be honored to be your mate, Kiara Moore."

Kiara reached down and grasped the sides of her skirt, lifting it so she could step over Cypher and stand immediately in front of Volcair. She took his hand. "We will be *best* mates."

Once again, that tingling sensation spread across his skin, intensifying the heat in his chest. Though he knew what she meant, part of him couldn't ignore what that word meant to his people. "What does it mean to be a *best* mate?"

She pursed her lips and scrunched her nose, looking up as though in deep thought. "I think it means *important*."

"So...it means we will be each other's most important friends?"

Kiara nodded, a solemn expression settling on her face. "Yes. We will be the bestest, most importantest mates ever."

Cypher inserted himself between their legs, clicking to make his presence known.

"He does not want to be left out," Volcair said.

"Cypher can be our best mate, too." Kiara patted the inux's head. "Do you want to see my room? I mean, I have to ask my mum if it's okay first because we'd have to take a car to get there, but I have the bounciest bed in the whole world, and it would be *so* much fun."

Volcair dipped his gaze to their linked hands. "Oh. Well, I do not think my father would let me leave the building right now. Besides, I promised him I would stay at this party for at least an hour."

"Yeah, I can't leave, either." Kiara pouted for a moment before brightening. "But we can go to the back room. It's where my backpack is."

Before Volcair could say anything, Kiara tugged him toward one of the food-laden tables. He couldn't find the will to resist her; part of him liked holding her hand too much to let go. Cypher darted back and forth between them, nearly tangling himself in their legs with each pass.

When they reached the table, Kiara released his hand. She stood on the tips of her toes, reached forward, and plucked a couple pieces of food from the spread—square-shaped items with colorful layers and leafy designs on top, cradled in little paper bowls. She held one out to him.

"One for each for us," she said.

He accepted the food, regarding it skeptically. "What is it?"

"Mum calls them *pee-teet fours*. They're my favorite. They're tiny cakes."

"Oh." Volcair wasn't sure what *cake* was, but he was willing to try. He lifted it to his face and opened his mouth.

"Wait! These are *dessert*. We can't eat them until later."

Volcair lowered his hand and furrowed his brow. "Why do we have to wait?"

"It would spoil our dinner." She glanced over her shoulder, leaned closer, and lowered her voice. "We have to sneak into the back room before we eat them, or an adult will stop us and make us eat some veg first."

"Veg?"

"Yeah, *vegetables*. Yucky green stuff, though some of it is more orange." She jabbed a finger toward another platter sitting at the center of the table.

Volcair tilted his head and studied the vegetables; they looked like cooked plants. He'd eaten many such foods on many worlds—even here on Earth—and had found most of them enjoyable. Was it possible these were simply of an inferior strain, or could only be appreciated by more sophisticated adult tastes?

He was inclined to believe Kiara, even if she was younger than him. This was her homeworld, after all, and she seemed earnest.

"So, do we just need the *cake*?" he asked.

"There's stuff from your people here, as well. Do you have a favorite? We can take some."

Volcair looked at the circular spread. The foods were arranged according to the culture that had produced them; he recognized the volturian portion, as well as the vorgal and terran sections. He walked around the table to the volturian food—followed by Kiara and Cypher—and nibbled his lower lip as he studied the offerings. She'd called the cake *dessert*, which he understood as some sort of after-meal treat.

"Oh! These are really good," he said, grabbing several kaanas off their tray. They were spherical treats large enough that he could barely fit two in his hand. Their exteriors had a clumpy, grainy look, but their insides were soft and gooey. He passed two of them to Kiara and took two more for himself.

Kiara turned her head to glance over her shoulder. "My parents are talking to some green guys right now—I think they're called vorgals." When she looked back at Volcair, she grinned. "But I like blue better. Are you ready?"

Volcair was suddenly quite aware of his pale blue skin. Heart beating faster than normal, he swallowed and nodded. The warmth in his chest hadn't subsided. Was this just what it felt like to be a normal child, or was it something more?

"Follow me," Kiara said. Clutching her treats close to her chest, she turned and broke into a run.

Volcair followed, struggling not to crush his treats as he dodged between tables and groups of guests. The adults barely spared the children a glance; for the first time, Volcair was glad for his effective invisibility. Cypher bounded ahead of them, stopping occasionally to loop back around so he wouldn't stray too far ahead.

Volcair found his attention repeatedly drawn to Kiara's bouncing curls; he didn't understand how hair could be so fascinating.

Kiara looked back at him as she neared an open doorway that led into a hallway. "Come on! Almost there."

She disappeared around the corner. Cypher lingered at the opening, staring at Volcair with yellow eyes.

Volcair hesitated for a moment and searched the room, picking his father out of the crowd. Vantricar, smiling his *I'm-everyone's-friend* smile, was standing with a pair of tall borians and a terran. Doing his *duty*.

Cypher bit down on Volcair's foot.

"Hey!" Volcair yanked his leg back. His stomach sank, and he turned back toward the guests, certain he'd just caused a scene and earned his father's disapproval. To his relief, none of them seemed to have noticed his outburst. Without wasting another moment, he hurried around the corner after Kiara.

He found her waiting just around the corner. She led him through a carved wooden door at the end of the hall. The lights turned on when they entered the room, revealing a large, rectangular table surrounded by fifteen or sixteen cushioned chairs. With gray-bordered white walls and three large windows on one side, the space was simple and somehow soothing. Stacks of cups, a basket of packaged food, and two machines Volcair wasn't familiar with sat upon a counter along one wall.

Kiara placed her treats next to a bright pink bag on the table. Once her hands were free, she pulled out one of the chairs and climbed onto it. She turned her dark eyes toward him, smiled, and patted the chair beside her. "You can sit next to me."

Volcair set his treats nearby Kiara's and pulled out the chair she'd indicated. Warmth flowed along his *qal* and spread across his skin, intensifying when his foot hooked on the leg of the chair as he moved to sit. He fell forward, catching himself with one hand on the table's edge and the other on Kiara's chair. His heart thundered.

Kiara grabbed his arm. "Are you all right, Volcair?"

He tightened his grip on her chair as his flesh hummed beneath her touch; it was like an electric current running through his arm, but it was pleasurable rather than painful.

She giggled. "You're glowing again. I wish my skin glowed like yours."

If his cheeks hadn't yet flushed, they did in that moment. "It is just...um... Well it is because..." He gently withdrew his arm, adjusted his chair, and plopped down onto it. He felt like the happiest fool in the universe. "Sorry if I bumped into you, Kiara."

"It's all right."

Cypher clicked, leapt onto the seat next to Volcair, and climbed onto the table. His paws tapped the tabletop as he walked to Kiara's bag, where he finally lay down. He cocked his head, crest feathers perked curiously as he glanced between Volcair and Kiara, slowly blinking his optics.

"I've never seen an animal like him," Kiara said, brushing her fingers along Cypher's side. "Oh, that's so cool! He feels like metal, but it moves like skin."

Cypher twisted his neck to nuzzle Kiara's palm.

Volcair leaned his arms on the edge of the table and tried—without success—to shake off some of the strange feelings inside him. "He is in the shape of a zeget right now, but he can change his form."

"He can *change*? That's amazing. Is a zeget something from another planet?"

"It is an animal from my homeworld."

"Are they your favorite animals?"

Shrugging, Volcair turned his gaze to Cypher. "I like them well enough, but...I think *Cypher* is my favorite. I usually let him pick what shape he wants to take."

"Mummy and Daddy won't let me have a pet, but if they would, I'd want a fox." She glanced at Volcair. "Do you want to see?"

"Yes." Volcair's orientation—hours of lessons about Earth from experts chosen by his father—had barely touched upon the planet's native wildlife, and fox had never been mentioned.

"Do you want to see, too, Cypher?"

Cypher bobbed his head excitedly.

Kiara grabbed her bag and dragged it closer, opening the flap. She pulled out several items, setting them on the table—a brush, small terran figurines, writing instruments, and a tablet. Sweeping the other objects aside, she positioned the tablet in front of her, turned it on, and flipped through its onscreen commands.

She smiled and tapped the screen. A three-dimensional hologram projected from the top of the tablet. "This is a fox."

The hologram depicted a four-legged creature with orange fur that darkened to brown and black on its legs. It had a narrow snout, large ears, and a bushy tail. There was something endearing about the creature—it seemed at once harmless and yet subtly mischievous.

Cypher eased closer, his snout nearly touching the hologram.

"I think Cypher likes it," Volcair said, smiling too; he'd smiled so much since meeting this girl that his cheeks hurt.

Kiara's bright eyes widened. "Oh! Can he change into one?"

Cypher tilted his head and looked at the terran girl, blinking slowly before he backed away from the hologram. He plopped down and rested his chin on her bag.

Volcair reached forward and rubbed between Cypher's crest feathers. "He is a bit...*shy* about changing in front of new people."

"Mates don't need to be shy around each other," Kiara said. "But that's all right. You don't have to change, Cypher. I like you just as well the way you are."

Cypher slid toward Kiara on his belly and nuzzled her hand. She giggled again.

The sound strengthened the warm sensation inside Volcair. Her happiness eased something within him—the bitterness he'd carried since his mother's death, the loneliness of his years of travel with his father. For the first time in his young life, Volcair felt like *himself*.

Clicking softly, Cypher stood up and stretched out. His scales rippled, and his entire body shook, seeming to expand and come undone for an instant. Kiara sucked in a sharp breath. Cypher dipped his head, and as he lifted it up, a wave ran along his spine, rearranging his shape as it went.

Volcair had seen the inux morph many times, and it always fascinated him, but all his attention now was on Kiara. He watched her expression change from startlement to wonder.

Cypher trembled, flattening his scales. His body was shaped like one of Kiara's foxes, though his ears were a bit too large and he had four eyes.

"Oh, thank you, Cypher. Thank you!" Kiara said. She leaned forward and hugged the inux.

Cypher rubbed his snout against her cheek affectionately before wiggling out of her hold. He walked back to the pink bag and quickly reverted to his prior form, curling himself around the bag as he lay down.

Kiara's excited expression did not fade. "Are you ready to try some cake, Volcair?"

He turned his attention to the treats they'd set atop the table. "Okay. How about you try a kaana, and I will try the cake. We can go at the same time."

"Deal."

They each picked up a treat and lifted it to their mouths.

"Ready?" she asked.

Volcair folded down the edge of the paper holding the cake. "Yes."

"Now!"

He bit into the cake. Its texture was an unfamiliar mix—the soft, crumbly, spongy portions in the middle were contrasted by the dark brown shell around them, which cracked and melted on his tongue.

The sweetness hit him a moment later. Volturian food often included a variety of plants and fruits, much of which possessed a natural sweetness, but this was a new sort of sweet, as overwhelming as it was intriguing. The melting outer shell complimented the softer middle layers perfectly, blending flavors and textures to create something unique.

"Mmm, this is yummy." Kiara took another large bite of her kaana.

Volcair licked the crumbs from his lips and tossed the remainder of the cake into his mouth. He hummed to himself appreciatively, emboldened by Kiara's response to the kaana;

Vantricar would not have approved of Volcair's table manners, but Vantricar was not here.

"This *pee-teet fours* was also delicious," he said once he'd swallowed.

"I knew you would like it! Do you want to play a game next?"

He folded the empty paper, careful not to dump the crumbs on the table, and set it down. "What kind of game?"

"I'll show you," she said, stuffing the remainder of the kaana into her mouth before grabbing his hand. She slipped off her chair and tugged him along.

Kiara taught him several games that were immensely entertaining despite their simplicity. His favorite was a game where one of them was *it* and had to tag one of the others; Kiara had proven surprisingly fast despite being smaller than Volcair, and Cypher's natural agility and size allowed him to easily avoid being tagged. Even when Volcair finally had to bend forward, settle his hands on his knees, and catch his breath, he was still laughing and smiling.

While taking a break from physical games, they used Kiara's tablet to make three-dimensional drawings in the air, which grew increasingly ridiculous by the minute. Before long, Volcair and Kiara were giggling uncontrollably at the slightest additions to their *artwork*.

He had no concept of how much time passed as they played; he didn't *care* about time.

Eventually, they returned to their chairs to eat the remaining treats.

"Um, Kiara?" Volcair frowned and glanced at the half-eaten kaana in his hand. "Can I...can I tell you something?"

"Of course. You can tell me anything."

"Well, it is just that I never...I have never had a friend

before, and I just wanted to say that I am glad you are my friend now."

Her eyes widened. "Didn't you have any mates on your homeworld?"

"I was very young when I left with my father. And we have traveled around so much…"

She smiled and placed a hand on top his; her skin was warm and soft. "I'm happy to be your mate, and I'll be your mate forever." Leaning toward him, she pecked a kiss on his cheek.

Heat flared in his face and crackled along his *qal*, and, for an instant, his heart stopped. Kiara's gesture seemed so innocent, but he could not understand it, could not understand what it made him feel.

It is probably just how terrans express friendship, he told himself.

But part of him didn't quite believe that. Years later, he would look back upon this moment and realize it was the instant he knew what she would be to him, what she would *mean* to him; he was simply too young now to pick up on it.

Cypher suddenly perked, his feathers fanning around his head in alertness.

The children both started when the door suddenly opened.

"There you are!" Jada Moore pushed the door wide as she entered. "We have been looking for you two *everywhere*."

Isaiah and Vantricar stepped inside behind her.

Kiara leapt off the chair to face her parents. "Volcair and I were just playing! We were having *so* much fun."

Isaiah glanced about the room, his lips downturned, before he shifted his gaze to Kiara and Volcair. "I can see that."

Volcair hurried off his chair and assumed a rigid posture as his father's attention fell upon him. His heart pounded; he couldn't read Vantricar's expression, couldn't tell if his father was upset or amused.

Jada moved closer to the table, which was scattered with crumbs despite the children's best efforts. "Oh, Kiara, how many sweets did you eat?"

Kiara clasped her hands behind her back. "Only a few. We didn't spoil our tummies."

"Next time, Volcair, tell me where you are going," Vantricar said, his tone as ambiguous as his expression. "There are forces in this universe that do not wish for our peoples to be friends, and when a child sneaks away, a parent's first thought is of danger."

"I am sorry, Father." Volcair bowed his head and averted his eyes. "My apologies to you, Minister Moore, and you, Lady Moore, as well."

"Ambassador Vantricar is correct. You worried us," Isaiah said.

Kiara frowned. "I'm sorry. It was my fault. I told Volcair to follow me and nick the sweets."

Volcair's cheeks warmed. Why was she taking full responsibility? "I am the one who wanted to leave the party, and I should have known better. It is not Kiara's fault."

A faint smile touched Vantricar's lips. "It seems our children have set an example for us—they are already friends."

Isaiah chuckled. "So it seems."

"*Best* friends," Kiara said. "Volcair is my best mate."

Volcair glanced at her from the corner of his eye and smiled. He didn't know what he'd done to earn such loyalty from her, but it made him feel good.

"Most of the guests are preparing to sit and eat dinner now. Would you two like to come and join us?" asked Isaiah.

Kiara clasped her hands together and raised them to her chin. "Could Volcair and I sit next to each other? Please?"

"I don't see why not," Jada said, lifting her brows as she glanced at Vantricar.

"So long as you both eat your *vegetables*." Vantricar settled his gaze on Kiara. "Your parents told me you do not care for them, but they are vital to your health."

Excitement lit up Kiara's face. "Oh, I will! I promise." She turned to Volcair and reached for his hand. "I'll even eat seconds if I have to."

Those delightful tingles ran up Volcair's arm when she laced her fingers with his, and something fluttered in his chest.

Best mates.

He knew Kiara really meant *friends*, but part of him wanted it to be more.

TWO

London, Capital of the United Terran Federation, Earth
    Terran Year 2080

"FATHER, WE *NEED* TO GO," Volcair said. He stood in the doorway of his father's office with Cypher pacing behind him.

"I am working, Volcair," Vantricar replied. "We will leave when I am finished."

Volcair clenched his jaw. "You knew the party was today. You knew what time it started. And now we are late because you could not set aside your work for a little while."

Vantricar's nostrils flared, and he stilled. "I do not appreciate the tone you have taken with me, Volcair."

"And *I* do not appreciate that I am failing Kiara because you cannot properly manage your work schedule!"

Slamming his hands atop his desk, Vantricar pushed himself to his feet. His *qal* glowed, sparking a furious light in his eyes.

Cypher whined and pressed himself against Volcair's calves.

Fear blossomed in Volcair's gut—perhaps he'd pushed too far—but that fear was not strong enough to overpower his frustration.

"I have had enough of your insolence, boy," Vantricar said with a growl.

Volcair refused to back down, refused to so much as flinch. "Then send me on my way with the driver. You can work, and my promise to Kiara will go unbroken."

"You are old enough to understand the importance of—"

"Of keeping promises. I have a duty to Kiara because I gave her my word that I would attend her birthday party, and you are preventing me from doing so. If your work is so important, Father, you can stay here. It is not as though you would acknowledge my presence once we were at the party, regardless."

Volcair had attended Kiara's birthday celebrations for each of the last four years, and he would not miss this one. Though the terran tradition of celebrating the anniversary of one's birth was meaningless to Volcair, it was important to Kiara, and that was all that mattered to him. She'd been particularly excited about this year—this was her twelfth birthday, which she'd said meant she was practically a lady.

Some of the fury faded from Vantricar's face, and he lowered his gaze. He said in a soft voice, "I have many duties to fulfill as well. You know this, Volcair."

Volcair's eyes suddenly stung. "What of your duty to me, Father?"

Vantricar's jaw muscles ticked, and his frown softened slightly, eased by a regretful shimmer in his eyes. He was silent for several seconds before he asked, "How late are we?"

"The party began thirty minutes ago."

Vantricar ran one hand through his hair while he dismissed his work on the desk console with the other. "Hopefully we have not insulted Minister Moore with our tardiness..."

A bitter taste spread across Volcair's tongue. He shook his head. "*That* is your concern?"

"I know you are infatuated with the minister's daughter, but you—"

"It is not an infatuation, Father."

"Oh? What, then, would you call it?" Vantricar walked around his desk and approached Volcair. "You are fascinated with this terran girl, and I will not dissuade you from it. But this infatuation will soon come to an end."

Volcair glared at his father. His heart pounded, and his mouth felt dry. "She will be a part of my life forever. I *love* her."

"Love? What do you know of love?" Vantricar came to a halt a meter away from his son, his expression hardening. "Have you grown so wise in your fourteen years you think you know what *love* means?"

Volcair hated how small he felt at that moment, but he would not show it. "I am old enough to know, Father. It is not your place to tell me how I feel."

"Now I understand why you asked me to obtain a balus stone." Vantricar's shoulders rose and fell as he drew in and released a deep breath. "You are young and confused, Volcair. This is nothing more than a phase. You will move on from it before long, and when you are old enough, you will find a volturian to mate. Of a respectable *qalar*, preferably."

"My *qal* reacted to her the first time we met," Volcair said, clenching his fists, "and it reacts every time I see her."

"The hallmark of a confused child," Vantricar replied, but there was a hint of uncertainty in his voice.

"I will give her the balus stone tonight, Father, and with it I will give my promise."

"I was ten years older than you are now when I gave your mother a balus stone and my promise. I did not tell you of that night so you could pervert it like this. This is too serious for you to understand while you are so young."

"I will do it all the same."

"You will do as I say. In six years, your time for service will have come, and you will take a civil position that will bring honor to our *qalar*. When you are ready, you will find your true *volturian* mate, and once you have garnered enough experience, you will join me in my work. It is what you are meant for. This time on Earth is a lesson in diplomacy with an alien species, *nothing* more."

Anger roiled within Volcair like a raging storm; it heated his skin and sent tremors through his limbs, made his gut churn and his chest tighten. Yet, why bother expressing that anger? Vantricar *heard* when Volcair spoke, but never *listened*.

"Can we leave, please?" Volcair asked.

With a heavy sigh, Vantricar lifted a hand and waved Volcair onward.

They arrived at the Moore residence fifteen minutes later—a full fifty-one minutes late. Hovercars lined the drive; there were likely *dozens* of guests in attendance, which would only make Volcair's lack of punctuality more pronounced.

Volcair hopped out of their vehicle—Cypher on his heels—before the driver had brought it to a full stop, slamming the door shut on his father's admonishments. His heart sped and his stomach knotted with anticipation as he hurried toward the manor's entrance.

Cypher bounded along beside him.

Strings of lights had been hung in the trees and between

the light posts along the drive, casting a yellowish glow in defiance of the deepening dusk. The doors to the Moores' large home stood open with a guard posted to each side, and small groups of guests moved in and out freely. Volcair and Cypher darted between two such groups on their way inside. Neither Volcair nor the inux were fazed by the glares they received from the adults, who seemed upset that the teenager hadn't stood aside in reverence as they passed.

The interior had been decorated with similar lights as the outside, their luminescence creating a brilliant new shine on the polished walls and floor. Though this was a child's birthday, most of the guests were adults clad in fine suits and dresses. Volcair recognized many of them from his father's diplomatic dealings. Gathered in little clusters, they chatted, sipped wine, and nibbled on finger foods from trays carried by servants.

It was everything Kiara said she disliked about such affairs, and everything her birthday parties always became—events only superficially celebrating her.

After a brief search, he found her in one of the large gathering rooms, standing with three other children—two girls and a boy, probably the offspring of terran officials with high-ranking posts. As always, though, it was Kiara who caught Volcair's full attention. The sight of her stole his breath. Each time he saw her, she looked a little older and a little more beautiful.

She wore a puffy white dress, and her hair—adorned with flecks of silver that shimmered under the lights—was pulled back into a tight bun. Though her lips were upturned in a warm smile, Volcair recognized the subtle, sad light in her eyes.

He had caused that sadness.

Volcair walked toward her. He would ease her mood, would show her that he'd kept his word, that he had come, that he would *always* come for her. But he drew to a sudden halt when the terran boy beside her reached for her hand.

Something ignited within Volcair, something hot and seething. He gritted his teeth and curled his hands into fists as a strange, thrumming energy coursed along his *qal*. His gaze locked on the boy's hand as it touched Kiara's.

The boy had no right to touch her, had no right to hold her hand. The contact was too forward, too familiar, too...*intimate*.

Kiara's brow furrowed. Her large, dark eyes dipped to the boy's fingers, which had wrapped around hers, but Cypher charged toward her before she reacted further. The inux released an excited warble.

"Cypher!" Kiara turned toward the inux, pulling her hand away from the boy's, and her face lit up. After a moment of searching the crowd, her gaze found Volcair's. Her smile widened, and joy snuffed out the sad light in her eyes.

The thrumming sensation along Volcair's *qal* continued, now accompanied by a familiar warmth.

My Kiara.

KIARA GRABBED handfuls of her gauzy skirt, lifted it up to provide a little freedom to her legs, and ran toward Volcair without a backward glance at the other human children. Her parents would've been appalled by her manners, but she didn't care.

"Volcair! You made it."

He opened his arms, and Kiara threw herself against him. He grunted softly at the impact but embraced her as tightly as she did him.

"Sorry I'm late," he said in English. His accent gave the words a unique flair.

"It's all right. You're here now."

She stepped away and tilted her head back to look up at him. Though he'd always been taller than her, he'd hit a significant growth spurt over the last year or so, and now had almost a third of a meter on Kiara. And lately, his height made her feel...*different*. She *liked* how he towered over her, how his arms engulfed her when they hugged. He made her feel protected, safe, cherished.

Her heart pounded so hard against her ribs that she swore it was about to burst free. Volcair was dressed in white Volturian formal wear, his tunic cut to emphasize his narrow waist. The high collar granted him an air of elegance, and his high boots and form-fitting pants made him appear even taller than he already was.

He was so *handsome*. Emily and Diane, the girls she'd just left behind, thought so, too; Kiara knew they were likely ogling him right now. They *liked him* liked him, and it always made her angry when they talked about him.

Volcair was *hers*, after all.

Just in case the other girls had any lingering doubts about that fact after Kiara and Volcair's embrace, she lowered her arms and took his hand in hers, lacing their fingers together.

"Kiara?" Edward asked from behind.

She glanced over her shoulder to see Edward approaching. She groaned.

"Who is he, Kiara?" Edward pressed.

Without another word, Kiara ran, tugging Volcair along behind her. She ducked beneath waiters' trays, dodged past conversing guests, and pretended she couldn't hear Edward as she hurried across the room. She laughed as excitement swelled in her chest, pushing her on faster. Volcair never lagged, never asked what she was doing; he trusted her. That felt good.

Finally, they reached the open back doors, beyond which more guests were gathered around tables in the garden. She stopped and released Volcair's hand only long enough to remove her heels and toss them aside.

"Kiara!" Edward called from somewhere behind.

She chanced another backward glance to see him on his toes, peering between the guests in the nearby room. She grabbed Volcair's hand and met his gaze. "We need to hide."

After casting a glare in Edward's direction, Volcair nodded and gave her hand a little squeeze. They raced outside and across the grass, passing beneath the string lights that had been hung around the grounds, with Cypher bolting ahead of them.

All three of them knew where they were going without saying anything. They crossed the tree line and entered the thick shadows beneath the boughs, barely slowing despite the darkness. They'd walked this ground hundreds of times before; Kiara knew the way by heart.

It wasn't long before they entered the small, grassy clearing where she and Volcair had spent countless afternoons—it was their secret spot, out of sight of the house and never visited by the groundskeepers.

Kiara looked up at the sky. Twilight had nearly given way to full dark, and the first stars, made tiny by distance, twinkled overhead. She took a deep breath as her heartbeat eased. The air here smelled green and alive, so different from the sterilized scent of the manor's gleaming halls or the stuffy offices in which her father conducted his work.

"Who was that boy?" Volcair asked.

Kiara wrinkled her nose. "Edward Berkeley. My father is friends with his, and they've been visiting lately. Often." She glanced at Volcair. "He *likes* me."

Volcair moved to stand directly in front of Kiara, brushing

his thumb along the side of her hand. "Did you...did you *want* him to touch your hand?"

"No. I don't like it, but he never listens." She reached up and tucked a strand of Volcair's blue hair behind his pointed ear. "You're the only one who does."

"If he touches you again, I'll break his nose."

Kiara laughed; she almost felt bad about her amusement, *almost* felt bad for wanting to see Volcair break the bloody little perv's nose, but it would serve Edward right to suffer a consequence for his behavior.

"You shouldn't do that," she said with a sigh. "It would look bad for you and your father."

Volcair frowned, and his eyebrows angled down over the bridge of his nose. "I don't much care right now. Bugger my father's reputation."

Kiara nearly chuckled—she usually did when he used words like *bugger*, which his accent made somehow pretty—but she knew this wasn't a laughing matter by his tone. She squeezed his hand. "Is everything all right, Volcair?"

"It is while I'm here with you. He just...he doesn't seem to understand, Kiara, that what *he* wants isn't what *I* want. He spends all his time busy with everyone but me, yet he expects me to follow in his footsteps. Sometimes I just don't want anything to do with him."

Kiara frowned and rubbed her thumb against his. "I understand. I feel like that with my parents sometimes, too. Usually they do that stuff because they love us. But just because they love us and they're older doesn't mean they're always right."

She released his hand and lowered herself onto the grass, sweeping the skirt of her dress beneath her to keep her legs covered. "But we're not worrying about that while we're here, right? Sit with me."

Volcair offered her a gentle smile and sat beside her. Cypher lay down with his body curled against Kiara's shins; she absently reached down and ran her hand along his back. No matter how many times she petted the inux, the feel of his skin was always a wonder.

This was what she'd longed for all day. Not the fancy affair, the crowd of strangers, the expensive gifts that were more about impressing her father than making her happy, or the children her age who she barely knew—who she didn't *want* to know. All she'd wanted for her birthday was some quiet time with her best mates.

Time with Volcair.

She tipped her head back. "The stars are already beautiful."

"They are," Volcair replied, "and I...I brought you one."

Kiara's eyes rounded, and she looked at him. "You did?"

Volcair leaned back, reached into his pocket, and produced a small box.

She smiled as delight filled her. "You brought me a present?"

"Well...technically, my father bought it, but it was my idea and I picked it out." Holding the box on his palm, he opened the lid.

A soft blue light shone within the case; it took Kiara's eyes a moment to bring the glowing object into focus. It was a teardrop-shaped stone wrapped in intricate white gold metal-work that connected to a delicate chain.

She gasped. "This is a star?"

"It's called a balus stone. But it kind of shines like a star, doesn't it?"

"It does." She couldn't believe how beautiful the necklace

was, couldn't believe he was giving it to *her*. She met his gaze. "Can you help me put it on?"

He carefully removed the necklace from its case. Its gentle glow made his *qal* markings even brighter than normal. Smiling, Kiara turned as he draped the chain around her neck. The brush of his fingertips over her skin sent a shiver through her just before he clasped the necklace in place.

"This comes with a promise, Kiara," he said.

Kiara settled her fingers on the pendant and turned to look at Volcair. "What kind of promise?"

"A promise that you'll always be mine, and I'll always be yours."

She inhaled sharply. Heat rushed to her cheeks, and butterflies fluttered in her belly.

"Truly?" she asked.

Expression solemn, he nodded. "Truly."

Keeping her gaze locked with Volcair's, Kiara leaned forward, and touched her lips to his. His eyes widened, and he gasped. Her heart stuttered.

Tingles of sensation bloomed outward from where their lips connected, filling her with heat—and with something pleasurable but indescribable. She closed her eyes. This was different from the kisses they'd shared before—the innocent, friendly kisses on hands or cheeks. This...this was a *real* kiss. His mouth was soft and warm, his breath fresh and clean with a trace of mint. She pressed her lips more firmly against his, relishing the feel of him, and let the kiss linger for a few more seconds before she pulled away.

She opened her eyes and looked at him again; his eyes were half-lidded, glowing brighter than the stone he'd gifted her.

He pressed his lips together, and his tongue slipped out a moment later, licking them. "Kiara..."

"I'll never take it off, Volcair. Ever. That's my promise," she said softly.

THREE

London, Capital of the United Terran Federation, Earth
    Terran Year 2081

VOLCAIR HALTED HIS PACING, turned toward the window, and braced his hands on the windowsill. He felt Cypher's optics on his back; the inux had been watching him from the bed the entire time, occasionally releasing concerned clicks. Volcair forced himself to look out over London, the city that had been his home for six years—longer than anywhere else, even the planet of his birth. He'd always found this place fascinating. According to the histories, it had been founded just over two thousand years ago, and it displayed that history proudly. The entire city was a blend of ancient and modern the likes of which he'd never seen.

Even now, at two o'clock in the morning, London was vibrant. There was always light here, sometimes in defiance of persistent gloom and gray skies, but this time of year always amplified the city's glow. There were new lights everywhere—

strung up across the streets, coiled around the bare boughs of trees, hung in windows, circling every light post. He'd learned long ago that winter was a time of holidays for terrans, more than he could keep track of. None of them meant anything to Volcair personally—but they were important to Kiara. That made this one of his favorite seasons.

But this year was different. Though London was as beautiful as ever, and there was an air of joy and festivity blanketing the city, it seemed hollow and flat to Volcair. What meaning could these terran celebrations hold while Kiara was away?

He turned his head to look at the tablet sitting on the nightstand beside his bed. Its screen remained dark. Cypher lay on the bedding nearby, head resting on his front legs with his optics still fixed on Volcair.

Volcair's heartbeat quickened a touch, and a tight, hot sensation—impatience of the highest degree—flared in his chest.

I should've pressed the matter with Father. Should've made him see my side, should've made him ask Minister Moore.

He knew at heart it wouldn't have made a difference; he'd recognized the finality in his father's tone when he'd made his request. Vantricar had refused to even broach the matter of Volcair accompanying Minister Moore's family on their trip to America. It went beyond Volcair's place being with his father, here at the intergalactic embassy. Minister Moore was going to America to conduct diplomatic business and fulfill some of his many duties to the United Terran Federation, and he didn't need another child underfoot to distract him.

It didn't matter that Volcair was a child only in his father's eyes—he was as tall as Vantricar now, and equally as broad-shouldered. He wouldn't have been a distraction to Minister Moore at all; Volcair knew how to give *adults* the space they needed to work. That was why he rarely spoke to his father most days—Vantricar was much too busy to deal with anything as unpleasant as his own child.

Volcair growled to himself and pushed away from the window, resuming his pacing. It was pointless to waste time worrying over his father. Kiara was all that mattered. Why hadn't she called yet? What was she doing right now? What did the city she was in—New York—look like? Did they have lights there like the ones here in London?

The tablet chimed.

Volcair darted to the nightstand, tripping over his own feet on the way. Cypher leapt back with a startled chirrup as Volcair caught himself against the bed and reached forward to accept the incoming holo call, unfazed by the fall—though his heart was thumping even quicker than before.

A hologram of Kiara from her shoulders up appeared above his tablet. Her hair was pulled back and held in place by a shining gold headband, her mass of springy curls wild behind it. Her lashes were long and curled, her lips painted a soft pink, and there were golden hoops in her ears. And there, around her neck, shining bright against her skin, was the balus stone.

She was beautiful.

"Kiara," he rasped, suddenly breathless.

She flashed him a wide smile. "Volcair!"

Cypher shoved his head in front of Volcair and clicked excitedly.

Kiara laughed. "Hello to you too, Cypher."

Volcair nudged the inux aside. He'd waited too long to talk to her, to see her, and he wasn't going to let Cypher hog the attention. Cypher rolled his eyes and clicked sharply at Volcair before flopping back down at the end of the bed with a huff.

Kiara chuckled again. "Did you miss me, Volcair?"

Warmth flooded his cheeks as he combed the fingers of one hand through his hair, tugging back the strands that had fallen into his face. He feared his grin was more embarrassed than suave now. "Just a little."

She gaped at him. "Only a little? Huh. Then maybe I should just say goodnight and hang—"

"No! No. Would it make you feel better if I said I was pacing restlessly for the last few hours waiting for your call?"

Kiara laughed. "It would, because I believe I drove my parents mad with how often I asked when I could call you."

Volcair smiled, pulled himself up, and sat on the edge of his bed, leaning toward the tablet. "Is that all you've been up to? If so, I'd still consider it productive."

She grinned and tilted her head. "No, Father's kept us busy. We toured New York City yesterday. I wish you'd been there with me to see it all. It was so lovely with all the lights up. Especially Rockefeller Center where they have their enormous Christmas tree. I also purchased a gift for you, too. The moment I saw it, I knew it was perfect."

"You didn't have to get me anything, Kiara." Still, her thoughtfulness made his *qal* warm.

Kiara tilted her chin down and raised her brows, giving him a look that clearly stated she would accept no argument on the matter. "It's Christmas." She chuckled. "Besides, I can tell from your *qal* that you're excited about it."

"I'm excited about seeing you when you get back. Christmas doesn't mean much while you're away. Anyway, that was yesterday. What have you been doing today?"

"We spent all day getting ready for this holiday party." She rolled her eyes. "It was bloody awful. Just all these boring ministers and government officials with their families, putting on their fake smiles and pretending to be happy to see every-one. It's exhausting."

She wrinkled her nose. "Edward Berkeley was there, too. He's always following me around. He kept asking me to dance, and to be polite, I danced with him—once! And I swear my toes will be bruised for weeks."

Fire sparked in Volcair's belly, and he clenched his fists. He wasn't sure what to be angrier about—that Edward Berkeley was in New York while Volcair wasn't, that Edward had pestered Kiara, or that the clumsy oaf had stomped on her toes. But Volcair's frustration wouldn't make any difference now; he wasn't there, and he didn't want to let such emotions spoil this precious time talking to her.

Cypher huffed, releasing a series of angry clicks. The inux didn't like Edward any more than Volcair or Kiara did.

"I suppose when you get home, I'll have to dance with you," Volcair said. "Just so you know how it's really supposed to go."

Her features softened, and she smiled. "I would love to dance with you, Volcair."

They'd danced before—often at the sorts of gatherings she'd described—but Volcair would never tire of it. Everything he did with her felt like it was the first time; the excitement and joy never faded. "Are you still due to return at the end of the week? I'll have to make room for that dance on my schedule. It's been quite full lately."

"As evidenced by your several hours of pacing tonight?" she asked with a smirk.

"I violated my schedule for you tonight, Kiara," he replied with a smile of his own. "You've kept me up quite past my bedtime."

"What time is it?"

"Quarter past two."

She laughed. "You're not even in your pajamas!"

Volcair leaned back to glance down at himself, chuckling. "Well, as I've said, I've been rather busy. It just doesn't have the same impact if you're pacing impatiently in your nightclothes."

"Shall we both get in our jammies, then? This dress is bloody itchy."

"All right, but make it quick. I need to rest up. I've a long day of staring out my window in tortured boredom ahead of me."

She laughed, set her tablet down—granting him a glimpse of her golden, lacy dress—and switched the feed to audio-only. Her holographic image vanished. "No peeking, Volcair."

Fortunately, her turning off the holo feed hid the way his *qal* flared in response to her words. He'd loved Kiara since the day he'd met her, long before he could've understood what that love would mean, and though he was still a bit uncertain about all the complicated things she made him feel, he couldn't deny that the way he looked at her had changed as they'd grown older.

The thought of her changing her clothes—of taking off that dress—was enough to heat his blood and make certain parts of him stir and ache to be touched.

Clenching his jaw, he forced himself off the bed and walked to the wardrobe standing on the other side of the room. He changed quickly, but his haste didn't make it any easier to ignore his arousal—nor did the fact that the silky, dark blue pajama pants he pulled on had been a gift from Kiara a few months before, a celebration of his day of birth that only she took part in every year. There was only one way he knew of to relieve the growing ache within him.

But that wasn't satisfying enough, and he didn't have the time now.

Whirring sounds and amused clicks came from Cypher, and Volcair turned his head to look at the inux. Cypher was staring at him, feathered crest raised, wearing a sharp toothed grin.

Volcair lowered his brows and narrowed his eyes. "Time to go, Cyph," he mouthed, gesturing toward the door.

Cypher made a whirring sound that signified his laughter before he leapt down from the bed and strolled to the door. As he passed Volcair, the inux turned his snout up and looked away. Holding his pants in place with one hand, Volcair quickly cracked the door open to allow Cypher out, closing it behind the inux as quietly as he could.

"Besides exhausting yourself with pacing because of how much you missed me, what else did you do today?" Kiara asked amidst the soft sounds of rustling fabric.

"If you think I did anything but wait for you helplessly," he replied as he tied the waist string of his pants, "then you seriously underestimate my dedication to you, Kiara."

"Come on, quit taking the piss," she said with a laugh. "Even Romeo wasn't that dramatic. What'd you *really* do today?"

He reached for the shirt that matched his pants but stopped his hand before he grabbed it. He hadn't missed the way Kiara looked at him when he was shirtless beside the pool, and he'd come to crave that cheeky stare from her. He turned and went back to the bed.

"Well, I had my usual lessons with all the overpriced tutors my father has employed. Today I began delving into the joyful intricacies of intergalactic trade associations. They let me out just before my brain began to fry, and I tried to take a walk around the city"—he scooped up the tablet and dropped onto his bed, sitting with his back against the wall—"but I the bodyguard my father has following me around is apparently uninterested in conversation. Thus began my pacing."

"Sounds utterly dull."

"Far less exciting than having Edward Berkeley step on my toes."

"I think I'd rather have jumped off the Statue of Liberty than dance with him for one more minute," she said, her voice sounding farther away.

Volcair smirked. "Now who's being overly dramatic, my little Juliet?"

"O Romeo, Romeo, wherefore art thou Romeo?"

He furrowed his brow. "I only spent a short time learning about terran literature...but wouldn't it be best if we *weren't* Romeo and Juliet?"

"You're right. They didn't end well. It'll be different for us. Are you decent?"

"At least half so. Not telling which half, though."

The hologram flickered back on. Kiara's gaze immediately fixed on Volcair, trailing slowly over his bare chest. There was a gleam in her eyes that had only started showing within the last year or so—and he felt its heat course along his *qal*. She'd left her hair up but removed the headband, and the makeup had been washed from her face, making the faint dark blush on her cheeks clearly visible now. This was Kiara at her most beautiful.

"Well, I'm not disappointed," she said, grinning.

She picked up her tablet and carried it across her room. Unable to help himself, Volcair dropped his gaze to her chest. She was wearing a thin strapped tank top, allowing him to see her delicate collarbone and the gentle slope of her small breasts. He swallowed hard and shifted on his bed as that ache resurged with new strength.

Kiara crawled onto her bed, set the tablet down next to the pillow, and lay on her side, facing him. She seemed to search his face for a moment before her smile faded. She reached up and grasped the balus stone, holding it loosely between her fingers.

"I miss you," she said softly after several seconds of silence. "Even though we're talking now, it's like I can feel the distance between us."

Volcair couldn't stop his smile from falling as well. "I feel it, too. But you're due back at the end of the week. It's not like we're going to be apart for years."

"I know," she sighed. "Lights off."

The light around Kiara dimmed, leaving only the glow of the hologram on her face and skin.

Sweeping back a few rogue strands of hair to tuck behind his ear, Volcair slid down to lay atop his bed, moving the tablet to rest on his chest. He especially felt the distance separating them in moments like this, when the hologram of her face looked so real, so close, that it almost seemed like he could lean forward and kiss her.

He needed a distraction from those feelings before they drove him mad.

"So, Kiara...when you're free of these obligations and don't have to travel around with your parents, what do you plan to do? What sort of life do you want to lead when you don't have to live this one anymore?"

Her lips stretched into a grin. "Does it get to include you?"

"I'd say it's a requirement that it includes me."

She chuckled. "Good." Her eyes turned up in thought. "My parents expect me to attend a university, and I want to go...but not to one of the places they'd choose. I don't need a prestigious school filled with the world's elite, and I don't want all the strict rules and attention that would come with it. I'll definitely never sit through another bloody diplomatic meeting again. In fact, I think I'll stay far, far away from any sort of government work." She looked back at him. "What about you? What do you want to do?"

"I'll have to enter mandatory service when I'm twenty, as the Dominion requires…but as much as I hate to ask him for it, my father has enough influence to obtain me a posting here on Earth with his staff. I'll gladly stomach that work to remain near you."

"It's so romantic that you'd face the torture of a bureaucratic posting just for me."

Volcair laughed. "Anything for you. And I suppose I'll just overlook that you didn't really answer my question."

Kiara arched a brow. "What do you mean? I answered."

"You more told me what you're not going to do than anything."

"And you didn't really tell me what you *want* to do, did you? That's more what you feel you must do." She nestled closer and released the balus stone, reaching forward as though to caress his cheek. Her holographic hand brushed only empty air. "As long as you're in my life, I don't care what I'm doing. Whether it means staying there in London, traveling the world, or going to worlds beyond the stars."

Chest tight, he lifted a hand and moved his fingers through hers; the contact produced not even the slightest sensation. Her holographic touch was even more empty than that of a ghost, good only for inducing a memory of what it might've felt like for their skin to meet. Volcair wished beyond all reason that he could travel through the tablet in that moment and find himself with her, in that faraway city, in the same room, just so he could smell her and feel the slightest of her touches.

The ache in his groin deepened with unfulfilled want, and he knew his *qal* was aglow just by the feel on his skin as he huskily replied, "I want the same."

Smiling, Kiara lay her hand on the bedding in front of her tablet and hummed softly. "My star. I love it when you glow."

Volcair's heart thumped as though to emphasize his next words. "For you, I always will."

FOUR

London, Capital of the United Terran Federation, Earth
   Terran Year 2082

KIARA STARED into the mirror and smoothed her hands down the front of her dress—her very *grown-up* dress. It wasn't poofy like the dresses she'd worn when she was younger, but a sophisticated garment like those her mother often wore—long and slimming, hugging her body up top with its loose skirt ending just below her knees. The square-cut neckline showed off her collarbone and the pretty necklace Volcair had given her for her birthday two years before. Kiara never took it off.

She turned to look at her profile. Though she'd grown several inches over the last few years and had lost the bit of chubbiness she'd carried as a child, she still didn't have the full, mature figure her mother possessed.

Kiara covered her small breasts with her hands and frowned.

Soon.

Soon, Kiara would be a woman, able to do as she pleased. But for now, she was a young lady with more growing to do—a young lady who'd be *fourteen* in a couple days.

Buzzing with excitement, she smiled widely as she turned her body to face the mirror.

What does Volcair see when he looks at me? Does he still see the little girl I was, or the young woman I am becoming?

Her heart pounded at the thought of him. Her best friend, her first crush—her *only* crush. He was meant to be hers. She just knew it.

No, he is mine.

Volcair had changed a lot over the years they'd known each other; he'd grown taller, his shoulders broader, features sharper, and hair longer. He was by far the handsomest boy she knew—probably the handsomest boy in the whole galaxy. Whenever she saw him, her belly fluttered, and she felt giddy, felt like she belonged, felt like everything was *right*.

A soft knock on her door startled her. She turned toward it as it opened.

"Kiara," her mother said, slipping into the room, "they're here. Are you ready?"

There was something heavy in her mother's eyes, something sorrowful in her expression.

Frowning, Kiara stepped closer. "Is something wrong, Mum?"

Jada cleared her throat and forced a smile. "Just come down. I'm sure everything will be fine. Volcair is anxious to see you."

Mention of Volcair turned Kiara's thoughts away from her mother's strange mood.

"They're early!" She squeezed past her mother and raced down the hallway toward the staircase.

"Kiara! You shouldn't run!"

"I know, Mum," Kiara shouted, but she didn't slow down. Clutching the bannister, she descended the steps quickly. Volcair usually met her in the foyer when he came to visit; he wasn't there now.

Jada hurried down the steps behind her. "Kiara!"

"Where is he?" Kiara asked.

"Outside, but—"

Before Jada could finish, Kiara ran to the tall double doors and darted through one before the doorman could open it fully. Anticipation thrummed through her as she surveyed the loop at the end of the drive.

There, standing in front of a long, black hovercar, was Volcair.

He stood with his hands in his pockets and his head slightly bowed, dressed in a suit that was a hybrid of volturian and human fashion—it mixed the stylized volturian collar and fabric with the sensibilities and fit of a traditional British suit. Such fashion fusions had become popular over the last few years.

And it made him look *very* grown-up.

Volcair glanced up. His frown rose into a smile that didn't quite touch his blue-white eyes when he met her gaze.

She sped across the drive, and he spread his arms to catch her as she slammed into him, wrapping her arms around his neck. She'd take away whatever sadness he felt. They always knew how to cheer each other up.

"You're here!" Kiara said, squeezing him tighter. "I thought you weren't visiting until this evening."

He tightened his embrace, as well. When he spoke, it was in lightly accented English. "I wasn't supposed to, but...something's come up, Kiara."

Kiara drew away from him and tilted her head back to meet his eyes. "What is it?"

Volcair sighed, and his frown returned. "There are new tensions between my people and the sedhi. My father has been reassigned to Arthos, where they are trying to mediate peace agreements."

"Well, your father is a good negotiator, isn't he? Everything should turn out fine."

"It means I have to go, Kiara."

His words—though none of them were complicated or powerful on their own—combined to freeze the entirety of the universe, leaving Kiara trapped in suffocating silence and stifling motionlessness for a second or two.

"What?" she asked breathlessly.

He *couldn't* go. He was supposed to stay here with her. They were supposed to grow up *together*.

"You'll be here for my birthday, right?" she asked, throat tight.

He didn't meet her gaze as he shook his head.

"Volcair?"

Kiara's chest constricted, her heart seized, and her lungs seemed to collapse, starved for air she couldn't draw in.

"The posting is considered *prestigious*." His jaw muscles bulged for a moment; he'd nearly spat that word. "We have to leave today. The *qalsarn* has demanded we go immediately due to the delicacy of the situation."

"*You* can stay here." She nodded as though that was the answer to it all. "We have plenty of room. You can stay with us."

"I cannot," he said softly. "I have to go, Kiara. And...I do not know when I will be able to return."

"No. No, you can't go. You *can't!*" Tears flooded her eyes, blurring her vision as she turned her head to seek out her mother, who stood a few meters away. "Tell him he can stay."

Isaiah, standing beside Jada, shook his head. "Kiara, my child—"

"Tell him!"

"Kiara, he can't," her mother said, placing a hand on Isaiah's shoulder. "His place is with his father."

"His place is with *me!*" Kiara's stomach sank, and sobs racked her throat. Her best mate, her Volcair, was leaving. She turned back to him.

Volcair had lifted his face. His features were hard, set in anger and determination. "I will come back some day, Kiara. We're...we're best mates, aren't we?"

Kiara wiped her cheeks and nodded. "The bestest."

He smiled, but the fierce light remained in his eyes. "Since I won't be here, I wanted to give you your birthday gift now."

Those words only made her more miserable. She didn't want a gift from him, she just wanted him here on her birthday, and the day after that, and the day after that. She wanted him here forever.

Volcair turned away from her and stepped to the waiting hovercar. He opened the back door, and Cypher leapt out in a shape he'd only taken on a few brief occasions—the graceful form of a large-eared fox, albeit one with metal scales and four eyes.

Cypher hurried to Kiara and stood on his hind legs, placing his front paws on her thighs. The series of clicks and whimpers he produced were more distressed than she'd ever heard.

She knelt in front of him and placed her hands on his sides. "You're not a zeget anymore."

"He wanted to change after I asked him to stay with you," Volcair said.

"What?" Kiara looked at Volcair. "You're...you're giving me Cypher?"

No! Her mind screamed that word over and over again. He couldn't do this!

Volcair nodded, and his nostrils flared with a heavy exhalation. "I can't stay, but he can. To be your companion and watch over you."

"But what...what about you? Cypher is your only other friend!"

"I guess that just gives me more reason to get back here eventually, right?"

Kiara shook her head and carefully let Cypher down as she stood. She ran back to Volcair and wrapped her arms around him, burying her tear-streaked face against his chest. "You can't go. I don't want you to."

He embraced her, rested his cheek atop her hair, and whispered, "I don't want to go, either, but I must."

"Kiara," her father said from immediately behind her, gently grasping her arms to pry her away from Volcair. "It's time, sweetheart."

"No! Please, Daddy!"

Ambassador Vantricar climbed out of the hovercar to stand beside his son.

Kiara met Vantricar's gaze as she struggled against her father's hold. "Please! Please, let him stay with us."

"That's enough, Kiara," Isaiah said, his voice soft but stern.

"I am sorry, Kiara," Vantricar said as he laid a hand on Volcair's shoulder. "It has been our greatest honor to come to know you and your family these past seven years, but duty calls us elsewhere. We must serve the will of the *qalsarn*, and through him, the will of our people."

Fury flashed in Volcair's glowing eyes. He bared his teeth and cast off his father's hand, striding toward her.

Kiara finally shoved away from her father just before Volcair took her into his arms. She clung to him desperately as he leaned his face closer.

When he spoke, his breath was warm against her ear. "Remember our promise, Kiara."

He turned his head. His cheek was wet when it brushed against hers, but he pressed his lips to hers before she could guess what the moisture was. She tasted him and something more, something salty, and dug her fingers into his back to take more of him.

The kiss was over far too soon; he drew his head back and met her gaze. It was only then she realized the moisture on his cheeks and the salty taste on his lips had been caused by his tears.

Her throat tightened. "Volcair..."

"Remember." He released her and stepped back.

She sagged forward; it was her father's strong arms that caught her and held her upright.

The raw emotion on Volcair's face, the pain and sadness, was more than she could bear to see, especially because she knew it was for her. Volcair only showed his true feelings to Kiara; he was usually quiet and reserved around his father. His open display only hammered home that this wasn't a jest. This was real.

This was happening.

"I will find my way back," Volcair said as he walked to the waiting hovercar.

Vantricar reached for his son, but Volcair batted his father's hand away. *Qal* glowing bright, Volcair looked at Kiara over his shoulder once before climbing into the vehicle. Vantricar lingered for a moment longer before following his son into the car.

The door closed with a thunderous slam.

Kiara's lower lip trembled. "Goodbye."

She stared at the departing hovercar until it was out of sight. Her father held her a little tighter, but his touch offered no comfort.

"Kiara," he said, "I know—"

Shrugging out of his hold, she turned and fled, racing back into the house, up the stairs, and into her room—barely noticing the clacking of claws close behind her. Once the door was closed, she let it all out—the pent-up pain, the loss, the sense of abandonment.

Her broken heart crumbled into a million pieces.

She threw herself onto her bed as she cried, tears flowing freely. Her throat burned, and it was hard to breathe, hard to feel *anything* but the growing emptiness torn open by Volcair's absence.

He's gone.

She clutched the blanket in her fists and buried her face in it.

Something leapt onto the bed beside her. A long, warm snout nudged her arm.

Kiara raised her head and turned her face toward Cypher. He whined, his eyes narrowing and taking on a sad tilt, before he lay against her. He settled his head next to hers.

Kiara wrapped her arms around him and held him close. "He's gone, Cypher. He left us."

Cypher produced a series of soft hums and clicks; she imagined he was trying to soothe her, trying to tell her everything was all right, that Volcair would be back.

Fresh tears spilled from her eyes. "He will come back, won't he? We'll just wait for him."

And she did.

She waited for him as days stretched into months, looking skyward every night to appreciate the stars that reminded her so much of his glowing *qal*. He was out there, somewhere.

Years passed, and she grew into a woman, marveling at the changes occurring before her own eyes.

How much had Volcair changed? Was he taller, broader? Had he let his hair grow longer, or had he trimmed it?

Did he think of her as much as she thought of him?

When she graduated school at the top of her class, the only face she wanted to see in the crowd was his, but there was no sign of him, no word. Yet she continued waiting.

She went to university, attended parties, made friends among her peers, and excelled in her classes, never giving up hope that he'd return soon.

Her heart broke a little more with each passing day.

Finally, after eleven years of waiting, eleven years of silence, eleven years of her parents urging her to live her life, Kiara finally gave up. She accepted the truth she'd refused to face throughout her youth.

Volcair was not coming back.

FIVE

*London, Capital of the United Terran Federation, Earth
    Terran Year 2094*

VOLCAIR DREW in a deep breath and released it shakily as the automated hovercar descended. His body thrummed with restless energy, and warm tingles coursed along his *qal*. The vehicle leveled at ground cruising height—just above the black, paved surface of the road—and continued forward. Though the trees, hedges, and fences lining the road must have changed over the years, this countryside remained familiar. He'd always been excited to make this trip as a child; now, he could barely contain his anticipation.

The hovercar turned onto a secluded lane with stone pillars on either side of the entrance. Volcair's heartbeat sped up. The branches of the towering trees flanking the lane grew together overhead, creating an arched canopy of wood and leaf that only allowed the sunshine through in little rays. The effect was one he'd always appreciated—it made the lane feel like a tunnel with a ceiling that glowed gold and green when the sun was positioned right, a place where shadows danced across the ground to create a whimsical air.

But as much as he'd appreciated that beauty, it wasn't the reason he had always been so eager to come here. There'd only ever been one reason he loved this place—Kiara. Volcair would've found even the barren gray dust of the Earth's moon a landscape of enchanting beauty if he had to traverse it to reach her. She enriched everything around her. Only thoughts of her, with the balus stone shining around her neck, had seen him through his long years of military service to the Entris Dominion. Those same thoughts would carry him through the remainder of his term.

The hovercar emerged from the tunnel-like lane and continued onto the paved circle at the end, coming to a stop in front of the Moore home. The outer walls, with their grayish-tan bricks, tall windows, and neatly manicured growths of ivy, looked exactly as it had the last time Volcair had seen it.

His mind flashed back to that day twelve years ago, and his heart stuttered. The tightness in his chest intensified, driven now by anxiety rather than eagerness, punctuated by a pang of guilt and a stab of bitterness.

The day he'd been forced to say goodbye to Kiara had been the worst of his life. He'd fought many battles during his service, had faced his own death—and witnessed the deaths of comrades—on many occasions, had seen blood and chaos, had known hopelessness and despair. He'd faced the death of his mother, who'd been his whole world, as a small child. He'd been forced to move repeatedly throughout his youth, never knowing a true home—though this place was the closest he'd ever come.

None of it had been harder than leaving Kiara that day.

None of it had affected him as powerfully. Not a day had gone by during which he hadn't thought of her in all that time, but circumstance had prevented him from contacting her. First it had been the rules of the Consortium, the rulers of Arthos, where his father had been posted by the Dominion twelve years ago. They'd forbid contact with species they'd not invited to join their city. Four years there had ended with Volcair being shipped back to Korous to officially enter his service.

Vantricar had expected Volcair to take a civil position within the Dominion government. Volcair had chosen military service instead. By now, he could admit to himself that part of his reason had been to spite his father, but the main motivation behind it had been respect for his mother. She'd been a commander in the Dominion military; this was a small way for Volcair to show that he remembered her.

But his decision to enlist had carried unforeseen consequences. His assessment upon enlistment had placed him immediately in a covert branch of the military—a prestigious but secretive posting that had sent him across Dominion space and beyond, that had seen him often operating deep within hostile territory. The work had been dangerous and thrilling, but it had also meant he was prohibited from communicating with anyone outside of ultra-secure military networks.

He'd effectively been cut off from the rest of the universe until now. Not that he cared about the rest of the universe —*Kiara* was his universe. She was all that mattered. And he'd been unable to contact her for twelve years.

He couldn't imagine the hurt it must've caused Kiara to go so long without hearing from him. The guilt had kept him up at night more times than he could count, eating away at his heart, whispering in the back of his mind. The way he'd had to leave was bad enough on its own, but having been unable to even send her a message in all the time since? Having never once been able to see her face as she grew into a woman, having never been able to hear her voice as it subtly altered with age?

Things changed over time. People changed. How different were he and Kiara now? They'd never seen one another as adults, hadn't talked in more than a decade. He knew he wasn't the person she remembered. What if she wasn't the person he remembered?

Bollocks. She'll always be my Kiara. Always.

...and I've been sitting here staring out the window in silence for at least a full minute.

Volcair hurried out of the hovercar, closing the door behind him, and stood up straight to draw in a deep breath of clean countryside air. The atmosphere of every place, of every world, had its own feel, but none could compare to this. It smelled—and felt—like he was finally home.

He smoothed the wrinkles out of his dress uniform and strode toward the front door. His stomach quivered and twisted, unable to decide whether he was eager or anxious, nervous or overjoyed. All those combat situations he'd weathered had been matters of life and death, but they seemed unimportant as he mounted the step leading to the home's entrance. This was far more dire a situation—it was a matter of love and destiny.

Clenching his jaw against his agitated nerves, he extended an arm and pressed the button for the doorbell. That familiar chiming sound—Kiara had told him it was meant to mimic church bells, though this lacked the same resonance and power —came from inside, muffled by the big double doors.

Seconds passed after the bell went silent, each more difficult to endure than the last. Volcair tensed his muscles to force them to keep still. He knew this sort of anticipatory energy too well, had dealt with it often over the years. Were he sitting, his legs would undoubtedly be bouncing, and he'd be fighting the urge to worry at his lower lip.

This was a moment twelve years in the making; the emotions welling up within him were too big to confront, too complex to decipher. He was going to see his mate, his Kiara, for the first time in what felt like an eternity. And he would spend the rest of his life trying to make up for having not spoken to her in so long.

The latch clicked, and the right door swung open to reveal Kiara's father.

Isaiah Moore's eyes widened. Regardless of what seemed unchanged outside the home, Isaiah served as proof that time left nothing untouched. The lines around his mouth and at the corners of his eyes were new, as were the white hairs sprinkled throughout his short hair and beard—the latter of which was also new.

"Volcair?" Isaiah asked incredulously.

Volcair offered a nod and a salute. "Good afternoon, Minister Moore."

Isaiah seemed to shake off his surprise. "Please, just Isaiah. I retired from my post several years ago, and you're an old friend of the family, regardless." He stepped aside, opening the door wider. "Please, come inside. It has been...it's been a long time."

There was a hint of strain in Isaiah's tone, something Volcair couldn't quite place.

"Thank you," Volcair said as he crossed the threshold. His eyes swept around the foyer; though the décor and lighting were exactly as he recalled, it seemed somehow smaller.

Isaiah closed the door and turned to face Volcair, looking him up and down. "The uniform suits you."

Far better than the career my father envisioned for me would have.

Volcair prevented himself from giving that thought voice, but only barely. This wasn't the time or place, and it would not do for him—especially wearing the uniform of an officer of the Entris Dominion—to speak so disrespectfully of his father to one of Vantricar's associates.

"Thank you," Volcair repeated.

"Come"—Isaiah gestured to an open doorway to the left of the front entrance—"have a seat. Would you like something to drink?"

"No, thank you." Volcair stepped through the doorway. The room had a couch and several chairs positioned around a dark, patterned carpet at the center. Only a few pieces of décor were on the walls, and most everything in the room was purely functional.

This had been introduced to him long ago as the drawing room. He'd been forced to sit here a few times as Vantricar and Isaiah chatted, both men often skirting around the business they truly meant to conduct while subtly positioning for the ongoing negotiations between the United Terran Federation and the Entris Dominion. Those few meetings had been the main reason Volcair had laughed when Kiara first referred to it as the boring room—though as they'd grown a little older, they'd changed the name to the bollocks room. Both seemed fitting.

Being in here now, as an adult, was an odd sensation for Volcair. Part of him still felt like a child called into a world of grown-ups; this wasn't his place, wasn't the environment he was meant to be in.

Isaiah walked to one of the chairs and seated himself, gesturing to the sofa as he did so. Volcair moved to the indicated spot and sat down. A nagging notion in the back of his mind suggested something was wrong here, something was off, and it was more than just Isaiah inviting him into this room—this room that had always been used, ultimately, to conduct business, however informally that business was sometimes handled.

"It's been a long time, Volcair," Isaiah said. "Twelve years or so, correct?"

"Indeed." Volcair struggled to keep his voice from sounding tight. He'd not come here for this, but he couldn't deny Isaiah this time. "Circumstances have kept me away from Earth for far too long."

"If I recall correctly, you must be in what, your seventh or eighth year of service?"

"I've just completed my eighth year."

"Nearly done then. Have you decided what you'll do when your term is over?"

I decided that years ago, and he knows it.

"I had planned to determine that with Kiara."

Isaiah pressed his lips into a tight line and nodded, but he did not reply.

"Is your daughter in, Sir? I'd hoped to see her. She's the only reason I've come to Earth during my leave."

Placing his hands on the armrests, Isaiah leaned back in his chair. The old leather creaked with his movement. "Kiara doesn't live at home anymore. She moved to a flat in Knightsbridge after university."

Volcair furrowed his brow. "Knightsbridge? Is that in London, or—"

"Yes. The West End, bordering Hyde Park. Lovely area. But it's best you don't go there, Volcair."

Heat suffused Volcair's face, and his anxiety quickly beat

back his eagerness, allowing dread to pool low in his gut. "Why?"

Isaiah's eyes were hard—with anger, it seemed, but also with something deeper, something more vulnerable. "When was the last time you spoke to Kiara?"

"The day my father took me away," Volcair replied in a low voice.

"That is why, Volcair. My daughter spent eleven years waiting for you. Those ought to have been the best years of her life, but she spent them *waiting*. Waiting for her life to begin." Isaiah leaned forward and shook his head. "Not a single word from you in all that time. Do you know what it was like to watch her joy dwindle? To watch disappointment grow in the eyes of my sweet, loving child? Imagine how it must've been for her!"

Volcair clenched his jaw as a resurgence of shame joined his dread, but there was something else in him now—fires of anger and frustration sparked in his chest. "My situation prevented communication before now. That's why I'm here. I came the first chance I had."

A hint of sorrow gleamed in Isaiah's dark eyes. "I understand. More than most humans, perhaps. I know what duty means to your people, and I have an idea of what's expected of you. But Kiara was very young when you left, and she didn't share that understanding. I don't think you did, either. Time has a way of seeming at once insignificant and impossibly slow when we are young, and I'm certain you had so many plans in place...

"But it's too late now, Volcair. She waited all that time without a word, without knowing whether you were dead or alive, and watched everyone around her live their lives. She finally moved on. She finally sought something more for herself. She's found happiness again."

"What does that mean?" Volcair rasped.

Isaiah leaned toward Volcair, settling his elbows on his thighs, bowed his head, and released a heavy sigh. The anger that had briefly given fire to his voice and posture seemed to have deflated just as quickly. "Kiara is engaged to be married."

Volcair's breath caught in his lungs, his heart ceased beating, and silence gripped the entire universe. Those words echoed in Volcair's head, devoid of meaning. Perhaps it was a matter of his grasp on the English language having deteriorated over the years. Perhaps he'd simply misheard. Perhaps there was some misunderstanding.

But even if he'd lost some of his knowledge of English, his translator implant would've picked up the slack, and the look on Isaiah's face—the sorrow and conflict—made it clear that this wasn't a misunderstanding. He'd said exactly what Volcair had heard.

Kiara is engaged to be married.

Volcair opened his mouth to speak, but only a soft, helpless sound emerged from his throat. The heat suffusing his face spread like wildfire along his *qal* to encompass his entire body. He couldn't tell if it was despair, anger, jealousy, or pain, and it didn't seem to matter. His lungs burned and his chest ached, and he couldn't draw in air, though he needed it desperately. He absently lifted a hand, clutching at the fabric of his uniform as though it could somehow alleviate his discomfort.

Isaiah reached across the distance separating him from Volcair and placed a solid hand on Volcair's shoulder, giving it a squeeze. "Breathe, Volcair. Nice and easy."

Volcair couldn't understand how he felt so empty and yet so impossibly full of churning emotion in those moments. He couldn't understand how his mind could be simultaneously blank and tumultuous. For twelve years, only one thing had been a constant, only one thing had been dependable—Kiara was waiting for him. Without that, *nothing* made sense.

He finally managed to take a quick, shallow breath, and followed it with a few more. "I... I just... To whom?"

Isaiah frowned. "His name is Daniel. They met at university, and were friends for a few years before she accepted that you weren't coming back."

"I was *always* going to come back."

"She thought that for a long time. So did I. But you didn't, Volcair." Isaiah released another sigh and tightened his grip on Volcair's shoulder just a bit. "I understand your duty to your people, but you have to make an effort to understand Kiara's position, as well. She was a girl when you left. You meant the world to her. Twelve years was nearly half her life. Do you understand the significance of that? How she felt trapped and unmoving while everything went on around her? How she felt alone despite the friends she had?"

Volcair gritted his teeth as his anger intensified. Even if he'd been unable to contact her, unable to return before now, he'd remained faithful. He'd never given up hope—hope had been the only thing to keep him going up to now.

"She made a promise to *me*," he growled. "Do you think I didn't feel alone? Even after days of fighting with little rest, I would lie awake thinking of her, knowing that she was out of my reach and that I was unable to change it. I swore I would return, and *she* promised to wait."

"And she was fourteen, Volcair," Isaiah said, unfazed by the display of anger. "She was a girl, and you were her everything, and when you left the light in her eyes dimmed. She tried to stay strong for so long, so much longer than I could have. But she was never the same with you gone. That's changed with Daniel. She's finally acting like her old self."

The fierceness of Volcair's anger recoiled from another stab of shame; it felt like his insides were flooded with chilling ice and consuming flames, opposing forces locked in a terrible, impossible balance.

Who was he angry at? Kiara...or himself? Who was more worthy of his rage—the one who'd waited for over a decade without any reason to hope but the promise of an immature, sixteen-year-old volturian, or the one who'd failed to send even a single word to her in all that time?

Volcair bowed his head, closed his eyes, and forced himself to take a deep breath. The air still burned his lungs and throat, and the tightness in his chest did not ease. "Is she happy?"

"Yes, she is." Isaiah withdrew his hand, and the leather on his chair creaked again as he shifted upon it.

Clenching his jaw, Volcair exhaled heavily through his nostrils. Hearing that she was happy hurt almost as much as everything else because *he* was supposed to be the one making her happy. More than ever before, he felt...untethered. He felt like his place in the universe was no longer set, like he was no longer connected to anyone, to anything. Like he'd simply drift through the void alone forever.

She was his mate. That had been an indisputable fact since the moment he'd met her, regardless of what Volcair's father had tried to say over the years. Kiara was his. But she'd chosen another. She'd moved on. He couldn't fault her for seeking happiness; if anyone could relate to that desire, wasn't it him, who'd spent so much of his youth moving from place to place and feeling disconnected from everything?

"She still has Cypher?" he asked; the words nearly stuck on his too-dry tongue.

Isaiah chuckled softly. "They have been inseparable. I had to have quite a few conversations with the headmistress while she was in school because she refused to leave Cypher home during class."

Despite everything, a tiny smile tugged up the corners of Volcair's mouth. His headstrong Kiara. Cypher was a part of Volcair...just like Kiara always would be. As long as she had Cypher, Volcair was with her, even if it wasn't in the way he'd always wanted. Even if it wasn't the way he'd always dreamed.

He'd asked too much of Kiara when he'd left Earth, hadn't anticipated the pain he would cause her by telling her to wait for him. Even now, he longed to ask Isaiah for her address, to have the driver take him to her flat, no matter how far the journey, so he could see her. So he could speak to her. So he could tell her that she was his, and that he wanted her—*needed* her.

But that she would have to wait even longer for them to be together.

And what would that accomplish? What if she didn't want him anymore? What if she truly was happy with this Daniel, and Volcair's sudden appearance disrupted that happiness?

Would he be able to bear the sight of her with another male?

Would he be able to bear the rejection?

His little smile faded even faster than it had come. He had endured so much to make it to this point, but the thought of her with another male—*happy* with another male—was too much. The thought of her joy being disrupted by his arrival was more than he could withstand.

Not ten minutes ago, he'd reflected upon the worst day of his life, the hardest day—the day he'd been forced to leave her. But he knew now he'd been naïve to think of it that way. *This* was the hardest day of his life.

This was the day he had to *choose* to let her go. The day he had to choose to let her have what happiness she'd found.

Opening his eyes, he forced his face into as calm an expression as he could muster—a task in which he succeeded only due to his years of experience on the battlefield, where his soldiers depended on him to appear confident and decisive no matter how he felt. Behind that mask was a different story; he was in a million pieces, and his heart had been pounded to dust. His limbs were weak and threatened to tremble, his mouth was dry, and his chest was constricted like it were caught in the coils of one of those large Earth snakes Kiara had shown him at the London Zoo many years ago. But Isaiah Moore didn't need to know about any of that. He was just a man who loved his daughter and wanted her to be happy.

Volcair had to follow that example—he had to do what was best for Kiara.

"I'm sorry for disrupting your afternoon, Minister Moore," Volcair said as he pushed himself to his feet. Fortunately, his legs accepted his weight, and his knees didn't buckle despite how ill he felt. "I'll take my leave. Please give my regards to your wife."

Isaiah's frown only deepened, reflected by the sad gleam in his eyes. "You don't need to leave so soon, Volcair. Please, stay for tea, or for dinner. Jada and I would love to have you."

Volcair didn't know what was worse—the invitation after what had just transpired, or the fact that he knew Isaiah was being sincere. "I appreciate the offer, but I must go. My leave is temporary, and there are only so many shuttles that will allow me to link up with the Dominion fleet. Good afternoon, Minister Moore. I'll...I'll see myself out."

He turned away and exited the drawing room before Isaiah could reply, moving at the rapid walk that had become his normal after years in the military. He didn't allow himself a moment's hesitation in opening the front door and moving through, didn't hesitate to send out a pickup call on his holocom once the door was closed behind him.

And he didn't allow himself a backward glance as he continued his brisk walk toward the tree-lined lane.

His Kiara had moved on. Volcair had to do the same; he knew if he looked back even once, that would be impossible.

SIX

Aboard the Trading Frigate Starlight
Somewhere in the outer fringes of Entris Dominion space
Terran Year 2101

HEART RACING, Kiara ran down the corridor, keeping one hand on the blaster at her hip. Her crewman, Tekel—a large, brown-furred azhera—ran just ahead of her, while Cypher kept pace at her side.

The *Starlight* quaked.

Kiara threw out her free hand, catching herself against the frame of an open door. If not for her quick reflexes, she would've stumbled face first into the wall.

"What was that?" she demanded, clinging to the doorframe as she righted herself.

"They just docked with our aft entry hatch," Umae, the *Starlight's* pilot, replied through Kiara's commlink earpiece.

"Bloody hell!"

Cypher skidded to a halt a few meters away and turned to face Kiara, staring at her with anxious, glowing eyes.

"Are they still blocking your signal, Cyph?" Kiara asked.

Cypher clicked and nodded.

"I want you to go hide and keep trying, got it?"

The inux narrowed his eyes and bared his fangs, clicking angrily as his scales scintillated and flowed like an angry ocean current. Kiara had no doubt that, were Cypher a person, he'd be telling her where she could shove it right now.

"Don't argue with me, Cypher. If anything happens, you're our only hope of getting help."

Cypher growled and stared at Kiara for a few more seconds before releasing a frustrated huff. He darted away.

"They've breached the airlock," Umae said, her husky voice panicked.

"That quickly?" Kiara asked, drawing her blaster.

Tekel was positioned at the closed door ahead of her, his long tail flicking back and forth as he stared through the door's small viewport. His blaster looked child-sized in his large, clawed hands.

Kiara fell into place opposite Tekel and leaned back against the wall. "How many?"

"Too many," Captain Mason Snider said through the comms. "Kiara…"

Growling, she adjusted her hold on the blaster and lifted her left arm to activate the holocom on her wrist. She flicked through the holographic menu until she accessed the ship's security feed.

Tekel had called them *pirates*, but their armor, weapons, and numbers were reminiscent of a small army. At least fifteen had already entered through the airlock, with more following. They advanced down the corridors with weapons readied.

There was no way the *Starlight*'s small crew—six people if Kiara counted herself—could fight off such a large, well-equipped force.

She had to make a choice.

"Mason, you're in command of this ship," she said, "but I think we should stand down."

"*What?*" Tekel snarled, glaring at her.

"I want you all *alive*. If we fight, they'll kill us. If we surrender, we have a *chance*."

"Better dead than taken," the azhera said. "Do you have any idea what they will do with us?"

Kiara clenched her jaw. The *Starlight* was the first ship she'd purchased when she started this business venture after university, and it remained her favorite. It had made the run between Earth and the Entris Dominion dozens of times, and she'd personally traveled on this ship for a good eighty percent of those trips, even after she'd expanded her merchant fleet. She'd always known piracy was a potential hazard of intergalactic trade, but her ships had remained untouched.

Until now.

"They're probably just after the cargo," she said, as much to convince herself as anyone else.

"Kiara, *we* are part of that cargo," Tekel replied.

"We *will* find a way to get help. Cypher is working to get a distress signal out, and if he can reach someone, he can act as a homing beacon. Still, it's your call, Mason. You know where I stand."

"Boss is right," Mason said through the comms. "Everyone fall back to the bridge immediately. Our only way out of this alive is by cooperating with our new *guests*."

"*Kraasz ka'val*," Tekel spat, slamming his fist into the wall. Kiara's translator offered no understanding of his guttural words. He pushed away from the door and ran alongside Kiara back to the bridge.

The rest of the crew was already gathered inside, fear in their eyes. Even the fierce borian, Umae, seemed subdued. Kiara's heart ached; these people were her friends, her family. If anything happened to them, she'd never forgive herself.

Please find help, Cypher.

She met Mason's gaze; he'd been with her since the beginning, and she trusted him to make the right calls when it came to the *Starlight* and its crew.

Though he wore a deep frown, he nodded to Kiara and said in a firm voice, "All right, everyone. Weapons away."

Kiara dropped her blaster into its holster. She didn't miss the crew's reluctance as they complied with Mason's order. Tekel and Umae seemed particularly riled—they both hailed from peoples with long-running warrior traditions.

Moments later, pounding footsteps sounded in the corridor outside the room.

"We surrender!" Mason shouted in universal speech, the most widely spoken language in the known universe. "We won't resist."

The door slid open, and the pirates stormed onto the bridge two at a time with blasters raised. They spread out around the edges of the room, partially surrounding the *Starlight*'s crew, who stood with their backs to the ship's control consoles.

A large, four-eyed tretin ducked through the doorway, barely clearing it. He was like a demon out of an old story, with two horns rising from his forehead and two more sweeping outward from the sides of his skull—and was probably close to two and a half meters tall including those horns. Black spikes jutted from his chin, matching the color of his long, black hair, and his lips were parted to reveal a mouth full of sharp teeth.

His long, powerful tail swayed behind him. He lowered his blaster and chuckled.

"Choosing the easy way?" he asked in a deep, gravelly voice. "The hard way is more fun, but this *is* more profitable. Take their weapons."

Several of the pirates moved forward, searching the *Starlight*'s crew and confiscating their weapons.

A male borian approached Peyton. The human woman—who'd always been introverted and timid but was amongst the best engineers in the business—whimpered and cringed away. The borian grabbed the back of her neck with one of his big hands and drew her closer.

"Got a few exotic *ji'tas* here, Vrykhan," he said.

Umae, a borian herself, spat at the pirate's feet. "You are a disgrace to our people."

The borian pirate drew a knife from his belt with his free hand and angled its point toward Umae. "But a *wealthy* disgrace."

Kiara growled and darted toward him, dropping a hand to her blaster. "Leave them alone!"

The big tretin stepped in front of Kiara, and she collided with him; it was like running face first into a brick wall. Before she could back away, he clamped a hand on her shoulder, his grip tight enough to nearly make her knees buckle. She cried out in pain; there was no doubt he could crush her bones to powder if he wanted to.

With his free hand, the tretin broke Kiara's hold on her blaster and plucked the weapon out of its holster. He passed it to one of the nearby pirates. Leaning down so his face was closer to hers, he ran the back of a clawed finger down her cheek.

"So soft," he said, trailing his finger toward her lips. When she turned her face away, he chuckled.

"Sod off, you knob-headed mingebag," Kiara said.

His grin widened. "So *spirited*. What does this look like to you, Brazzik?"

The male borian glanced at Kiara. "Merchandise, Vrykhan."

"*Unique* merchandise," Vrykhan replied. "These soft ones are terrans. Very rare and in high demand." He dropped his gaze to Kiara's chest and grabbed her jacket with his free hand. "I think I can see why."

Tekel lunged at the tretin.

One of the pirates slammed the butt of his auto-blaster into Tekel's face, knocking him aside. "Don't you fucking move!"

Vrykhan's long, pointed tongue slipped out from between his sharp teeth and ran along his dark lips.

Kiara punched him in the face and hammered her elbow onto his forearm, hoping to dislodge his hold on her, but Vyrkhan made no indication of pain—his head moved a centimeter, his arm not at all. He tightened his hold on her shoulder. Kiara's legs gave out as fresh pain jolted through her, but his grip was so strong that he held her upright.

He swung her around, slammed her back into the wall, and tore her jacket open like it was made of paper.

"Well now, what is this?" He hooked a claw beneath the chain of her necklace and lifted it off her collarbone. "A balus stone? You let one of those Dominion worms rut you in exchange for this?"

Kiara pressed her lips together and stared at the pendant.

Vyrkhan curled his fingers around the stone.

Don't.

The tretin yanked on the necklace. For an instant, the

chain bit painfully into her skin, and then it snapped, producing a flare of stinging pain on the back of her neck.

"No!" Kiara thrust out a hand to reclaim the necklace, but Vrykhan lifted it out of her reach.

He tossed the pendent to Brazzik. "Hold on to that. Those things sell well enough that it's worth fencing with the rest of the cargo." Looking back at Kiara, he grasped her chin and turned her face from side to side. His hold on her was firm, punishing. He finally released her shoulder to brush the tips of his claws through her hair. "Such a pretty thing. You'll earn me a lot of credits."

Vrykhan shoved away from Kiara, forcing her against the wall again and knocking the air from her lungs. She stumbled forward, but Tekel—blood trickling from his cat-like nose—forced his way over and caught her by the upper arms to steady her before she could fall.

"I want the merchandise moved into the cargo hold and this ship's systems up and going," Vrykhan commanded. "Set course for Caldorius. We'll offload everything in one go."

Several of the pirates slung their weapons over their shoulders and hurried to the ship's control stations as the others herded Kiara and the crew toward the door at gunpoint. Tekel helped Kiara walk; her legs remained unsteady.

Kiara glared at Vrykhan. "You will face justice for this."

"And you'll face a miserable life of slavery, my little pet, probably sucking off some wealthy merchant's stem for the rest of your years," the tretin replied. "Should've died fighting."

"Ship is low on fuel, sir," one of the pirates called. "Its course was locked for the nearest refueling station, Janus Six. They already checked in as making their approach."

"That's a Dominion station," another said.

"We divert the course, and they'll come looking," Vrykhan grumbled. "How far will this ship make it on its current stores?"

"Just far enough to leave it stranded in space. It won't make the meet-up location or Caldorius, that's for sure."

Vrykhan growled. "Brazzik, stay aboard with a small party. Match their species"—he jabbed a finger at Kiara and the others—"as closely as possible, and keep a few in the hold to guard the goods. Stop, refuel, and move on. This haul's too valuable to lose. Start moving the merchandise as soon as you get to Caldorius, but keep the terrans. They'll fetch a premium price, so I'll have to contact the right purveyors...though the ertraxxan might be interested in one of these. He said he's looking for something exotic."

"Bastard," Kiara muttered, wishing she could blast those bloody teeth out of his skull.

"Do not fuck this up, Brazzik," Vrykhan said. "Get there in one piece, and you can have a go at the female borian."

Brazzik grinned.

"Yaril, stick with him. We'll find you on Caldorius after I've met with Cullion," Vrykhan said.

A reptilian ilthurii nodded and moved toward the control consoles.

"Move it," one of the pirates growled, jabbing the barrel of his blaster into Kiara's back to shove her along.

Tekel tensed, sticking alongside Kiara as she staggered forward. She felt his claws extending; he eased when she placed a hand on his forearm. Mason wrapped an arm around Peyton's shoulders, holding her close, as Umae and the female volturian, Inara, glared at their captors.

Kiara released a heavy breath through her nostrils and turned her face forward as she and her companions were ushered off the bridge. Had she made the right choice? This way meant they'd probably live, that they had a chance...but if an opportunity for escape didn't come up soon, what sort of lives would they be forced into?

Come on, Cypher. We're counting on you.

COMMANDER SYNTRELL VOLCAIR Vantricar held in a sigh and resisted the urge to pinch the bridge of his nose as he reviewed yet another ship's manifest. He'd chosen to renew his military service after earning the right to carry the name of his ancestral *qalar*, and he'd done so knowing his rank could eventually mean a focus on administrative duties despite—or even because of—his exemplary combat record. The leadership of the Entris Dominion often *rewarded* its most decorated soldiers with positions considered safe and easy, like Volcair's current command of Janus Six, a Dominion-operated space station. Though the station was important as a potential base of operations for Dominion fleets and served as a checkpoint and refueling station for private trade vessels traveling in and out of Entris space, life here was monotonous.

Every day during his six months commanding Janus Six had seen endless perusals of shipping manifests, security clearances, and requisition forms to keep the station—which was not unlike a city floating through the vacuum of space—adequately stocked to provide for its garrisoned soldiers, long-term residents, and passing travelers. The crises he dealt with were not matters of life and death, but of keeping congested shipping lanes flowing, of mediating between angry merchants and rival crews, and of delivering justice to the diverse people who passed into his jurisdiction.

He often caught himself yearning for simpler times—for the black-and-white reality of combat.

For the life he'd briefly led on Earth so many years ago.

"What is the situation with this one?" he asked as he brought up the next manifest.

"Trade frigate registered with the United Terran Federation," Lieutenant Beltheri, who stood near his desk, replied. "It is pre-cleared, en route to Deduin. One of the docking guards flagged it. Suspicious behavior from the crew."

Volcair grunted; *suspicious behavior* was a common reason for his soldiers flagging docked vessels. Most of the time, nothing came of it—some of the commercial crews were in deep space for months-long stretches and were in understandably deteriorated emotional states when they arrived. But sometimes there *was* more; the Dominion was not without enemies and malcontents.

He scanned the ship's information. The *Starlight*, port of origin on planet... Volcair straightened in his seat.

Earth.

Not surprising; Earth was the terran homeworld, and the United Terran Federation had only colonized a handful of worlds thus far.

His throat constricted as he manipulated the file to show the registration information.

OWNER: *Kiara Zuri Moore*
Terran; UTF Citizen
Licensed for trade in UTF and Entris Dominion Territories.

. . .

FINGERS SUDDENLY NUMB, he touched the control on his uniform's breast to activate his commlink. "This is Commander Volcair. Who flagged the terran ship?"

Lieutenant Beltheri furrowed her brow.

After several seconds of quiet, the comm crackled to life, and a male said, "It was I, Commander. Ensign Korian Malthan."

"What did you see, Ensign?"

"Two of the ship's crew disembarked to engage the refueling process and present their official manifest, Commander. They seemed impatient and anxious beyond reason."

"No recorded distress signals," the lieutenant said, preempting Volcair's suspicion. Pirate hijackers were known to take hostages to persuade captured civilian crews to get stolen ships through checkpoints unhindered, but it was too soon to assume such a case here.

"Was one of them a female terran? Dark hair and brown skin?" Volcair asked. His heart thumped as hard as it had during his first combat drop.

"No, sir. A borian and a volturian," Ensign Korian replied.

Volcair leaned forward, propped an elbow on his desk, and dropped his forehead onto his hand. Kiara was the vessel's owner, but that didn't mean she was on board; countless ships were owned by individuals who never set foot upon them.

But there was a chance she *was* aboard the *Starlight*. And if she was...

Was she avoiding him? Was her crew in a hurry because she'd instructed them to get the ship out of the station as quickly as possible, thus eliminating any chance of seeing Volcair?

The very thought of it hurt, but thoughts of Kiara were

always bittersweet. He'd been so sure about his relationship with her for most of his life. So sure their paths would meet again, and that when they did, they'd be forever intertwined.

Fate had decided otherwise years ago.

If she is here, I must *see her. Just one more time.*

And he could not discount the possibility, however slight, that the ship had been overtaken by pirates. In that case, anyone aboard—including Kiara—was in danger. Even the most infinitesimal chance of that was too much for him to take.

"What is the *Starlight*'s current departure status?" he asked.

"On hold, sir," replied Lieutenant Beltheri, "pending your approval."

Flattening his hands on the desk, Volcair pushed himself to his feet. "I will speak with the crew personally."

Beltheri frowned and said, "Respectfully, sir, we have several more cases to review, and—"

"I will attend this matter personally," Volcair said. Anxiety churned in his gut, but he forced it down; he needed closure. He needed to know she was happy. Needed to know she was safe.

Once she'd departed from Janus Six, he would let himself feel the pain of losing her anew—a pain that time seemed unable to heal.

Beltheri bowed her head. "Yes, sir."

Volcair stopped in front of the lieutenant on his way to the door. Beltheri was a good soldier despite her relative lack of experience, and he had no doubt she would earn many honors during her service, but she was only a few months out of the officer's academy—she undertook every task with a strict adherence to the rules, just as she'd been taught.

It was an admirable quality, but she would have to learn flexibility eventually—especially if she was ever deployed in combat.

"You have my leave to continue reviewing the flagged manifests, Lieutenant. I trust your judgment."

Beltheri lifted her chin and stiffened her stance to attention. "Thank you, sir."

Volcair nodded and exited the room. The seemingly endless number of responsibilities tied to his command faded for the first time since he'd come here, giving way to thoughts of Kiara. Excitement sparked in his stomach, mixing with his anxiety and creating something new, something nauseating and uncertain and uplifting.

He knew what he'd feel when he saw her—*she is meant to be mine, my mate, my forever*—but it wasn't the truth. It hadn't been for years. She had moved on.

And he feared he never would.

Volcair proceeded through the corridors at a brisk pace, offering hurried return salutes to the soldiers he passed. The journey from his command center to the bay in which the *Starlight* was docked wasn't a quick one under normal circumstances—though Janus Six was remote, it was large—but his anticipation made it feel even longer than usual despite his haste.

He took a military-use-only shuttle to the docking bay and hesitated as he was crossing the upper catwalk. Kiara's ship was there, docked with its aft portion inside the bay's protective forcefield. It was a Thrassian-class frigate—a terran version of a popular volturian cargo ship, blending the volturian flare for style with a human practicality.

Just one more time...

Volcair descended the steps and strode toward the

Starlight. Massive metal docking arms held the ship in place. That sparked a pang of guilt in his chest; would she think he was holding her prisoner? Was that what she'd thought when she found herself a new mate back on Earth, that she was finally freeing herself from promises made before she was old enough to know any better?

He climbed the ramp to the ship's aft entry door and drew in a deep breath.

We were children when last we saw one another. We have both changed. Whatever we thought was between us...it was just innocent friendship.

Volcair was unconvinced by his own reasoning.

He lifted a hand and pressed the button on the control panel marked *CALL* in terran letters.

The small screen above the button flickered on, and a male borian with chiseled features appeared on it.

"Yeah?" the borian asked.

"I am Syntrell Volcair Vantricar, the commander of this space station."

The borian's eyes widened slightly, and he glanced at something beyond the edge of the video feed. "And? What do you want?"

"I need your crew to disembark."

"Look, we're on a tight schedule. We, uh..."

Another individual appeared on the screen—a dark-skinned volturian from the Kolduran *qalar*, by her violet-red markings. "We're on a tight schedule, sir," she said, glaring at the borian. "Cargo isn't going to deliver itself."

"And we haven't done anything wrong. Our manifest is all in order," the borian added, earning a sharper look from his companion.

Volcair kept his expression neutral; he understood Ensign Korian's suspicions now.

"I need the two of you and the rest of your crew to come to the aft entry and disembark." Volcair raised his left arm to access his holocom. He kept it low, hoping it was out of view of the camera relaying his image to the people inside the ship, and flicked his fingers through the control screen to send a message to Lieutenant Beltheri.

Need a boarding crew standing by, DB9-14.

The borian and the volturian exchanged a glance before the former grumbled, "Fine."

The screen beside the door went dark. Volcair switched off his holocom and waited, the sense of dread in his gut thickening with each passing moment. Either Kiara *really* didn't want to see him, she wasn't here, or...

With a long hiss, a rumbling, and the whir of unseen motors, the airlock door released and swung inward. The interior door of the small chamber beyond was already open; the borian and the volturian stood in the doorway.

"Where is the rest of your crew?" Volcair asked.

"We're it," the borian said.

The female volturian frowned. "The others are *resting*. We've had a rough trip so far."

Volcair shifted his gaze between the two. Something darted across the corridor behind them—something silvery and low to the floor. A moment later, a familiar inux peered at Volcair from just within one of the side doorways, revealing only two of his eyes, part of his narrow snout, and one large, backswept ear.

Volcair's heart skipped a beat, and his breath caught in his throat. He hadn't seen Cypher—the only creature in all the universe he considered a true friend apart from Kiara—for nineteen years. Why was the inux acting so skittish?

It took all Volcair's willpower to keep from outwardly reacting to the unexpected sight. He lifted his arm, activated his holocom, and summoned the ship's manifest. "You have how many aboard?"

"Seven," said the borian.

"*Six*," replied the volturian.

Expressions darkening, the pair glared at one another.

Volcair was suddenly aware of the holstered blaster on his belt but dared not lower his right hand toward it.

"I see. There are six listed on the manifest for this trip." He clicked his tongue, watching from the edge of his vision as Cypher silently crept into the hallway and approached, metal scales standing up and vibrating as though in alarm. "I will need to speak with the owner of the ship. If there is an error on the manifest, it will need to be resolved before we can move you into the departure queue. This sort of thing happens often."

"He's not on board," the borian said. "He, uh...he backed out at the last moment. Other business. Above our paygrade. That's why I was confused for a second."

Volcair frowned and dismissed the holocom's projected screen. "Oh. That is unfortunate. I will have to have my team contact the owner to straighten this out. That can take some time from this deep in space. If I could have you and your fellow crew members disembark..." He stepped backward, turning so he stood perpendicular to the borian and the volturian, and gestured to the bay floor behind him.

Neither crewmember moved; their gazes were hard and calculating, the gazes of people who regularly faced death and no longer knew how to flinch away from it.

A familiar calmness settled over Volcair. He'd been here before, many times. For a long while, he'd thought he liked this state because it was simple—either you survived, or you didn't —but he knew better now. It was the *emptiness* he had appreciated. He didn't feel that emptiness now; Kiara would not leave his thoughts, and a thousand *what-ifs* spiraled through his mind.

Volcair slowly shifted his right hand to his blaster, keeping his gaze locked with the individuals before him. "We will get this sorted out as quickly as possible."

Everything moved in a sudden burst of speed. He drew his blaster as both crewmembers—pirates, undoubtedly—reached behind their backs to pull blasters of their own. Volcair fired the first shot, hitting the borian in the chest in the same instant that Cypher, scales shifting to form long, wicked spikes, leapt at the female volturian.

She screamed as Cypher slammed into her back and fired several wild shots that hit the floor, ceiling, and wall. Volcair stepped back and squeezed the trigger of his blaster again, hitting the borian—who was still on his feet—in the neck.

The female fell, writhing and thrashing to dislodge Cypher.

An alarm blared in the docking bay.

"Alert! Shots fired in docking bay nine near gate fourteen," declared a computerized voice through the overhead announcement system.

With a choked grunt, the borian dropped. Volcair turned his blaster toward the downed volturian, intending to fire, but she was already still. Her blood glistened on the metal floor paneling.

Cypher reverted to his prior form—that of Kiara's favorite animal, the fox—and looked up at Volcair.

Releasing a heavy breath, Volcair activated his commlink.

"We have hostiles on the *Starlight* with a potential hostage situation. I need a strike team down here immediately."

As the comms lit up with chatter, Cypher stepped off the dead volturian and hurried to the borian, pawing open a pouch on the pirate's belt. Keeping his blaster ready and an eye on the corridor, Volcair crouched beside the inux.

Cypher backed away, tugging something out of the pouch with his teeth.

It was a white gold chain with a familiar pendant attached to it.

Volcair's chest constricted. He held out his hand, and Cypher lowered the balus stone necklace onto Volcair's waiting palm.

If Cypher hadn't been evidence enough, this was all Volcair needed to know Kiara was here. Was she safe, or had she been harmed?

He closed his hand around the necklace. Under different circumstances, he might have wondered why she still carried the balus stone after she'd chosen a path separate from him years ago. Why would she still have it when she'd already taken another male as her mate?

But with Cypher and the necklace here, all he could think about was Kiara's safety. There were undoubtedly other pirates on this ship. Kiara had to be somewhere on board, too. There were soldiers inbound, but it would be at least a minute before they arrived, and that wasn't soon enough. Not when Kiara was in danger.

"Take me to her, Cypher," he commanded as he rose.

Cypher stalked forward, and Volcair followed the inux through the interior airlock door, taking a two-handed grip on his blaster.

Fear roiled in the back of Volcair's mind—fear for Kiara, the girl, the *woman*, who was supposed to be his mate. The woman he'd taken too long to go back to.

"How many more pirates?" he asked as they neared the end of the corridor, where a doorway opened into a perpendicular passage.

Cypher's scales rattled, his color darkening for a moment. While most of his scales reverted to their normal silver, one section remained dark for a few seconds—in the shape of the terran numeral *seven*. Cypher flatteened himself on his belly and shimmied forward. He paused just before the entry into the next hallway and raised his ears.

Heavy footsteps sounded from around the corner, and someone shouted in a gruff voice, "Brazzik! Falka! What the hell's going on out there?"

Volcair halted several paces from the entryway and dropped to one knee. He aimed his blaster at the opening.

"Moerg," a voice called through the ship's overhead comm system, "there's a soldier in the aft entry corridor!"

At the same instant, a burly azhera with a tangled mane and an auto-blaster in his hands stepped into the doorway.

The azhera—presumably Moerg—met Volcair's gaze as Volcair fired. The blaster's high whine was amplified in the relatively tight corridor.

Moerg grunted, flinching back as the first bolt sizzled through his shoulder. Volcair's immediate follow-up shot struck the left side of the azhera's chest. Maintaining a one-handed grip on his auto-blaster, Moerg squeezed its trigger and sent a burst of plasma bolts into the wall. Flecks of molten metal splashed at Volcair, who thrust himself aside to avoid the stinging debris. He fired again as he fell against the wall.

Volcair's third shot landed between the previous two, and the azhera crashed to the floor.

"Commander?" Lieutenant Beltheri said through the commlink. "Commander, the boarding team is inbound. They will breach in two minutes. Please fall back to await reinforcement."

Volcair glanced down at Cypher as the inux walked around the fallen azhera and entered the next corridor.

"Get the *merchandise* out of storage," said the voice on the ship's overheads. "We need some meat shields."

If the pirates were allowed the chance to hide behind hostages, this would become a prolonged incident almost guaranteed to end in the loss of innocent life; Dominion protocol did not favor negotiation with criminals, outlaws, and terrorists, even in these circumstances. It was a desperate move on behalf of the pirates—which meant Volcair needed to make his own desperate move, no matter how stupid or dangerous it was. He *had* to press on alone.

Not alone. Cypher is here.

Cypher looked back, meeting Volcair's gaze, and nodded.

Volcair shoved himself to his feet and advanced, hesitating only long enough to fire another bolt into the azhera's head before he followed Cypher into the left branch of the next corridor. They soon arrived at a recess in the hallway's corner which contained a ladder leading down to a lower level.

The inux halted at the edge of the opening and glanced over his shoulder at Volcair, producing a series of soft clicks. Then Cypher bounded forward, scales flickering as his front paws elongated into hook-like talons to grab hold of the rungs. He descended out of Volcair's sight.

"Open the door and get them out," someone said from below. "You heard Yaril. We got company."

"Knew this was a bad idea," another person said. "Should've just towed this thing."

There was a loud, reverberating clang on the lower deck, followed by a deep rumbling. Volcair knew the sounds well—a heavy-duty cargo hold door was being opened below. The noise was an opportunity—it could mask the sound of his movement —but it was also a dire warning.

He was running out of time.

Volcair didn't bother with the ladder; he dropped into the opening and landed heavily on the metal floor three meters below. The jolt of the impact shot up his legs and clacked his teeth together, jarring his balance. He caught himself against the wall. Cypher brushed against his boot, coiling slightly around his shin. Volcair had forgotten how reassuring the inux's presence could be.

The voices from the corridor—which was at least twice as wide as the one above—were made indistinct by the sound of the opening door.

"Only six left, right?" Volcair asked. He stepped into the corridor before Cypher could respond.

The wide passage was divided into several sections by partially closed, sliding double doors—the sort that would auto-matically close to seal compromised compartments in the event of a hull breach. It was a standard safety feature on many space vessels. Each section had its own large cargo bay door, all marked with terran letters and numbers. The bay door closest to the ladder was rumbling open now.

One pirate—a green-skinned vorgal—stood at the door's control panel, his left hand on the switch while his right aimed a blaster into the widening gap. Two more pirates stood between the door operator and Volcair, one of whom was watching the bay door.

The other was watching the ladder access from which Volcair had just emerged.

The pirate made eye contact with Volcair and shouted, "Spawn of a skeks!"

Volcair fired; his enemies did the same. Plasma bolts zipped down the corridor in both directions.

Diving into the only available cover—the recess containing the ladder—Volcair flattened his back against the wall. Plasma pierced the metal around him and darted past the opening. With such limited cover—and so outgunned by his enemies—it was only a matter of time before he was hit.

And it was potentially a matter of moments before the pirates dragged out their *merchandise* to use as living shields.

The bay door clanged again and went silent; it had opened fully.

He sank down into a crouch, and Cypher moved up to nuzzle his thigh. Volcair showed him the holocom on his wrist. "Can you interface with this?"

The inux's eyes flickered; he nodded.

"Do it. And climb up on my right shoulder."

Cypher hopped nimbly onto Volcair's shoulder, his paws creating almost painful focal points through which his weight pressed down on Volcair's flesh; though small, Cypher was heavy.

Shifting his grip on the blaster, Volcair opened the holocom's projection screen. "I need you to patch through a camera feed from one of your optics and extend that optic along the barrel of my weapon."

Several plasma bolts burst through the wall overhead; Volcair muttered a curse and ducked lower.

Cypher laid himself over Volcair's shoulder with a series of low buzzes and clicks, stretching himself along Volcair's arm. His scales rippled, and those around one of his optics peeled back. The electronic eye extended outward on a thin, segmented tristeel wire, trailing over Volcair's forearm and the back of his hand to settle on the rear sight of the blaster. The holocom screen changed to a two-dimensional video feed—a view from Cypher's perspective down the barrel of the blaster.

Keeping low, Volcair turned to face the wall. He extended his right arm to move the blaster into the corridor, watching Cypher's optic feed.

Two of the pirates had moved behind the large compartment doors, leaving only their heads and arms exposed to shoot in Volcair's direction.

Volcair wasted no time; he fired rapidly, adjusting his aim to correct the trajectory of his shots, which were made more difficult by his skewed, indirect perspective. Whether they thought Volcair was firing blindly or couldn't resist the tiny target he'd presented them, neither of the pirates ducked behind the blast doors to protect their heads.

The pirate on the left caught a plasma bolt in the face and dropped. The other went down when his weapon was struck by one of Volcair's shots and its power cell detonated, causing a small but powerful explosion that blasted the pirate's smoking corpse backward.

Volcair stood up and cautiously emerged from his cover, slowly advancing along the corridor. Only the vorgal remained unaccounted for, and there was only one place he could have gone.

Ice flowed through Volcair's veins.

"Hop down and give me eyes in that room, Cyph," Volcair whispered as he neared the opening.

Cypher slid down and, despite his weight, landed silently on the floor. The inux kept low, nearly crawling on his belly as he crept to the open bay door. Volcair split his attention between the optic feed and his immediate surroundings.

One of Cypher's optics snaked around the doorframe and into the bay to reveal a huge chamber filled with neat rows of crates and transport containers of varying compositions and sizes. A group of aliens with bound arms was kneeling amongst the smaller crates not far from the door—a male azhera, a female borian, a female volturian, and three terrans.

It was one of the terrans who commanded Volcair's attention—a tall, brown-skinned female with dark, curly hair and big, brown eyes. Though he hadn't seen her since she was a fourteen-year-old girl, he couldn't ever have mistaken Kiara for anyone else. He recognized her like they'd only said goodbye yesterday. She was more beautiful than he remembered, more beautiful than he'd imagined possible.

And the vorgal pirate stood behind her with his arm around her neck and the barrel of a blaster against the side of her head.

"Vanguard team has entered the aft airlock," said someone over Volcair's commlink. "Commander, what is your location?"

"Cargo hold, aft cargo bay. Secure the upper deck," Volcair replied.

The pirate holding Kiara stared at the bay door with wide, panicked eyes.

A last, desperate move, Volcair reminded himself.

"Sending a squad to assist you, Commander."

"Negative," Volcair replied. "I have a delicate situation here. Secure the upper deck; we have at least three hostiles at large."

There was too great a chance of the nervous pirate harming the hostages if he was confronted by a Dominion strike team.

Volcair lowered his left arm and tapped on the wall lightly. When Cypher looked back at him, Volcair switched off his commlink transmissions, sank into a crouch, and beckoned the inux closer. Cypher retracted his extended optic and padded to Volcair.

"Have to move quickly. Use the containers as cover to get behind him," Volcair whispered.

Cypher nodded.

Volcair advanced to the edge of the doorway with Cypher directly in front of him. "I am the commander of this space station," he called.

"I'll shoot her," the vorgal shouted.

Glancing down, Volcair watched through Cypher's feed as the inux peered around the corner again.

Baring her teeth, Kiara struggled against her captor's hold. The vorgal pirate shifted his attention to her as he wrestled her back. Volcair tightened his grip on his blaster, forcing himself to remain in place, and nudged Cypher's flank with his boot.

The inux darted into the cargo bay, crossing the small open space to take cover in the rows of crates and containers.

"I am your only chance to negotiate a way out of this," Volcair said, monitoring Cypher's progress on the feed. "Harm any of these hostages, and you will not walk away."

"You think I'm afraid to die?"

"No. But I think you do not *want* to die, which means we can work this out."

Kiara was in the next room, only a few meters away, but Volcair couldn't see her, couldn't touch her, couldn't know she was okay. The thumping of his heart resonated throughout his body.

Hurry, Cypher.

"Think I'm going to fall for that? I agree to any deal you give me, and there'll be a Dominion hit squad waiting for me at the other end."

The images on the holocom screen shifted wildly as

Cypher went through a series of turns. When it stabilized, the inux was looking down a long row of crates—the pirate stood at the end, still clutching Kiara, his left side in profile to Cypher.

Cypher crept to the right side of the aisle—where he was most likely to remain outside the pirate's field of view—and stalked forward.

"That does not need to be the truth," Volcair said. He held his breath as Cypher closed to within a few meters of his target.

"You Dominion worms are all about honor until it comes to dealing with anyone outside your system. Then you lie through your damned teeth."

"I promise you," Volcair said as Cypher's feed wobbled and drew back slightly, "there will be no hit squad in your future."

Cypher leapt at the vorgal, front legs outstretched. His claws sharpened into four-centimeter-long talons an instant before they sank into the back of the pirate's thigh.

The pirate screamed, and Volcair, blaster raised, rounded the corner.

Cypher dangled from the back of the pirate's leg, kicking his back paws to shred the pirate's pants and the flesh of his calf beneath. Blood streamed from the open wounds. Kiara wrenched herself out of the pirate's hold and fell forward. The female borian shifted aside, breaking Kiara's fall with her own body.

Volcair pulled the trigger three times as he advanced. Each bolt found its mark in the center of the pirate's chest. Cypher disentangled himself from his prey just before the vorgal collapsed backward.

Switching his commlink back on, Volcair hurried to the bound hostages. "I have secured the hostages in the cargo hold, aft bay. Vanguard, you are free to sweep the entire ship."

He meant to survey the *Starlight*'s crew for injuries, meant to ask if they were hurt, if anyone was unaccounted for, but his eyes met Kiara's first, and he froze. Warmth blossomed across his chest and swept along his *qal*—a sensation he'd not felt in nineteen years, a sensation part of him had hoped wouldn't come if he ever met her again.

It was the answer to a question that had haunted him since he was sixteen years old, and it was the answer he'd feared.

He *couldn't* move on from Kiara.

SEVEN

A torrent of emotions swept through Kiara—surprise, disbelief, joy, desolation, abandonment, regret—as she stared into those familiar, faintly glowing white-blue eyes. Years of heartache flashed through her memory one at a time, each more impactful than the last.

And despite all that, she couldn't stop the growing swell of happiness within her.

Volcair was a man now, his features chiseled and sharpened by the years. His shoulders were broad, and his tailored uniform suggested a lean, athletic body beneath. His slicked-back blue hair was disheveled, hanging to his shoulders with several rogue strands dangling over his left eye.

She trailed her gaze over the markings on his face; how many times had she stared up at the night sky, seeking to trace those same patterns in the stars?

But it was his eyes that kept drawing her attention. His eyes —harder, sadder, *lonelier* than she remembered—that called to her soul. She knew those eyes, even after so long. He had grown, and his body had changed, but the Volcair she'd known so well in her youth was still in his eyes.

"Volcair?" she asked breathlessly.

His lips parted, but it was a few seconds before he said, "Kiara."

Tekel grunted. "And I'm Tekel; that's Umae, Inara, Mason, and Peyton. Now that we've all been introduced, could you stop staring at each other and release us?"

Kiara blinked, shook her head, and looked at the *Starlight*'s crew. They were all on their knees, arms bound behind their backs, save Umae, who lay on the floor propped on her elbows; she'd used her body to catch Kiara.

Cypher leapt over the nearby corpse and charged toward Kiara. Blood glistened on his scales.

Despite the gruesome scene, she couldn't suppress a grin. "You did it!"

He brushed against her side, tail twitching as he released excited clicks and whirs.

Volcair stepped over to Kiara and crouched, taking hold of her arms to help her onto her feet once Cypher moved aside. She found herself wishing she wasn't wearing her jacket just to feel his hands on her skin. He assisted Umae afterward, and quickly set about removing their bindings while Cypher cut the ties around Tekel's thick wrists.

Several sets of footsteps sounded in the corridor. Kiara tensed and instinctively dropped her hand to her hip, reaching for a blaster that wasn't there. Tekel stepped in front of her and spread his arms. His claws extended from his splayed fingers.

"It's okay," Volcair said in English, settling his hand on Kiara's shoulder with an odd hesitancy. "They're friendly."

A moment later, four armored soldiers carrying autoblasters entered the cargo bay, each with the symbol for the Entris Dominion—letters in flowing, circular Volturian script—on their shoulders.

The foremost soldier turned to Volcair and bowed his head. "Ship is secure, Commander. We eliminated three more hostiles on the bridge."

Volcair nodded, switching back to Volturian when he said, "Excellent work. Call in a clean-up crew, and put the medical bay on standby. I want these people checked by a medic and made as comfortable as possible."

The soldier bowed a little deeper. "Yes, sir."

Two of the soldiers stepped forward and freed Kiara's remaining crewmates.

Volcair turned to face her fully, and so many emotions crossed his face at once that she couldn't decipher any of them. His expression eased to something more neutral after he released a slow breath.

"We have some space in the officers' quarters," he said. "I can take you and your crew there, at least for a while, so you can settle down. I... We will have questions. About the pirates."

"Of course. Thank you," Kiara said.

"Was there a tretin on board?" Mason asked, rolling his shoulders once his arms were free.

"Negative," replied one of the soldiers.

Volcair frowned, and the muscles of his jaw ticked. "There was a tretin?"

"His name was Vrykhan," Kiara said. "He told his crew to take us to Caldorius to be sold, and that he'd join them after he met with an ertraxxan."

"Vrykhan," Volcair echoed. "He is the most wanted criminal in this quadrant of Dominion space." His eyes roved over

Kiara from head to toe and back again. "Come. My soldiers will handle the situation on your ship."

VOLCAIR TOOK his leave after bringing the *Starlight's* crew to the medical bay. Though Kiara knew she shouldn't have been hurt by his sudden departure, she was. She told herself it was duty that pulled him away, but she couldn't help wondering if his strangely withdrawn attitude had something to do with it; did he *want* to avoid her?

After Kiara and her crew were examined and cleared by the medic—thankfully suffering nothing more than some minor cuts and bruises—they were brought to the officers' quarters, where they were each assigned their own room. The soldier who'd escorted them said they were cleared by the commander to stay as long as it took for any investigations regarding the hijacking to be conducted.

Cypher preceded Kiara through the door to her room, leapt onto the bed, and curled into a ball as he lay down. His scales gleamed silver, having been scrubbed clean of the blood that had coated him after the rescue.

Kiara smiled. She'd never been prouder of the inux. He'd always been a wonderful companion, her closest friend, and today, he'd helped saved the lives of Kiara and her crew.

Kiara crossed the room and set her belongings on the desk that stood against the far wall. She shrugged off her jacket, draped it over the chair, and tugged the hem of her tank top out from her pants. She raised a hand to her collarbone. Her necklace was gone, and she felt naked without it. Kiara had worn the balus stone every day for twenty-one years, even while she'd been engaged to Daniel, and the one time she'd removed it willingly, she'd felt like she'd done something terribly, indescribably *wrong*; it had made her sick to her stomach.

She sighed heavily and pressed her hands to her face as bitter tears stung her eyes.

I didn't do anything wrong.

But why had it felt like such a betrayal?

Because I broke my promise.

No, that's not fair. I waited eleven years. He never sent word, never came back. I had a right to move on with my life.

But she never had moved on, had she?

Seeing him now not as the beautiful boy she remembered but as a man brought all those old feelings back to Kiara. Her heart still beat erratically in his presence, her blood still warmed at the sight of him. He'd only grown more handsome over the years, just as she'd known he would.

There was a knock on her door.

Wiping her eyes, Kiara turned toward the door.

Cypher raised his head and clicked.

"Relax, Cyph," she said. "It's probably Mason or Tekel."

Taking in a steadying breath, Kiara pasted a smile on her face, walked to the door, and opened it. The air fled her lungs.

Not Mason or Tekel.

Volcair stood on the other side of the doorway, dressed in a dark uniform that was tailored to his athletic frame. When his eyes met hers, his *qal* glowed a little brighter.

My star.

"Kiara. I wanted to make sure you were well, after what happened."

Heat suffused her, pooling low in her belly. Even his voice had changed; it was deeper, smoother, more sensual.

"Great. I'm...great. The medic cleared us no problem, just

some minor bumps and scrapes." She cleared her throat. "Though, uh, you probably already knew that."

"Yes, but..." Volcair's eyes fell to her bare shoulder, where Vrykhan's viselike grip had left the nastiest of her bruises, and he frowned. "A medical exam cannot account for all the wounds these situations inflict."

Kiara smiled lopsidedly. "Hazard of the job, right? I'm fine, though. Really. No one was seriously hurt. That's all that matters to me."

"May I enter?"

"Oh! Uh, yes, of course." She moved aside, and Volcair stepped past her. His scent filled her nose—clean, exotic, and all *him*. She closed the door once he was clear of it.

Cypher jumped down from the bed and bared his teeth in what Kiara had always thought of as a grin. He hurried to Volcair, stood on his hind legs, and settled his paws on Volcair's thighs as he made a series of excited clicks.

Volcair patted Cypher's head, keeping his back toward Kiara.

Cypher closed his eyes and nudged Volcair's palm with his snout.

Crouching, Volcair ran both hands down the inux's sides, smoothing over the silvery scales. Cypher excitedly waggled his foxlike body and nuzzled Volcair's chest, producing soft hums and clicks as he soaked up the attention. It went without saying that Cypher had missed Volcair.

I missed him, too.

Kiara stepped closer to Volcair. "So...a commander, huh?"

"Yes." Volcair gently guided Cypher down, rose, and turned to face her, his shoulders stiff. "And you are the proprietor of a trading company?"

"I am." Kiara stopped about a meter away from Volcair and

glanced down as Cypher brushed against her legs. She bent down and ran her palm along the inux's back. "It was never something I imagined myself doing, but I felt like I needed to... reach for the stars, I guess."

With a final, undulating series of clicks, Cypher walked to the bed, jumped atop it, and lay down. He watched Volcair and Kiara with his ears perked but his head down.

Kiara tilted her head back to meet Volcair's gaze. Her heart quickened; he was breathtaking. Unable to resist any longer, she raised a hand and—without hesitation or restraint, just as she'd done so many times as a child—touched the *qal* on his cheek, tracing the markings with her fingertips. They flared with blue light.

"You are still so beautiful," she said softly.

Volcair took in a sharp breath and caught her wrist in one of his hands. "Kiara..."

His grip, while not painful, was firm. Something in his reaction, in his tone, seemed like a warning, seemed like *rejection*. He'd never stopped her from touching him before.

"What's wrong, Volcair?"

"I cannot bear to taste what I cannot have," he replied.

Kiara's brows fell as she frowned. "What do you mean, Volcair?"

Without releasing his hold on her wrist, he dipped his other hand into his jacket pocket. When he lifted it, her necklace— the balus stone pendant he'd given her for her birthday twenty-one years ago—dangled from his fist. A wave of relief struck Kiara; she'd thought the necklace lost forever when the tretin had snatched it away.

"Why do you still have this?" Volcair asked.

Kiara looked from the necklace to Volcair's eyes, which shone with a cold light. "Because it was a gift from you."

"Does he know?"

"Does *who* know?"

"Your mate!" Volcair's grip on her arm tightened for a moment before he released her and stalked away. "The male you chose to be with. Does he know you carry the favor, the *promise*"—he lifted the necklace and shook it—"of another male?"

Kiara, stunned to silence by his sudden outburst, could only stare at him with her lips parted in shock. Volcair had never raised his voice to her, much less in anger.

"And now to touch me like this, to tempt me..." Volcair shook his head. "You have a duty to the one you chose, to honor your bond. You shame him—and yourself."

Her shock and confusion gave way to a spark of irritation. "What the bloody hell are you on about, Volcair?"

He lowered his arm and turned away from her. "I thought of you every day after I left, even when I was deployed to the farthest reaches of space. *Every* day. And when I found out you had moved on...I tried to move on, too. Tried to stop thinking about you. It never worked. But as much as I have always wanted you, I have always known you were better than to betray your mate—whether that man was me or not."

Kiara's body trembled in fury and disbelief. "You *what?* Are you...are you seriously standing there, after all these years, calling me unfaithful?"

"You lay your hand upon me and smile sweetly, while—"

"I don't have a mate," she snapped. "And you would've known that if you had ever come back!"

He looked at her, brows low, jaw tense. "I did. And your father told me you were engaged."

Kiara flinched, and everything inside her froze in that moment. He'd gone back? He'd gone back to Earth and spoken to her father? She'd always trusted her parents, and that trust only amplified the sense of betrayal she felt at that moment; why hadn't her father told her?

Why hadn't Volcair gone to *her*?

"And you didn't think to speak to me?" she asked quietly, turning her face away from him.

Cypher's ears were folded back. His scales flicked and rolled in agitation, but he remained silent as his glowing eyes shifted between Kiara and Volcair.

"What could I have said?" he demanded. "You had made your choice."

Kiara squeezed her eyes shut as though it could transport her somewhere else. Though her anger hadn't yet dissipated, her growing despair—cold, thick, and painful—was overtaking it. "I waited years for you. *Years*. I didn't hear a single word from you in all that time, and you never came back. Eventually I understood you never would come back. It's true that I tried to move on. I was engaged to a man." She opened her eyes and met Volcair's gaze. "I *slept* with that man."

Volcair's skin paled, but his markings burned with a new intensity.

"And it felt like a betrayal—like I was betraying *you*." She jabbed a finger at the necklace clutched in his hand. "That was the first and only time I took off that necklace since you gave it to me. Even though I hadn't seen or heard from you for twelve years, I still felt like I'd betrayed you when I tried to make love to the man I was going to marry. So I didn't marry him, because all I could think of was you. *You*, who never came back for me." She lowered her arm. "I made the choice to try and live my life, but you chose not to seek me out. If you had chosen different, I would have, too."

"While I was in Arthos with my father, we were prohibited

from contacting species who hadn't been integrated by the Consortium. And then I had to fulfill my duty to my people, Kiara. I was sent on covert missions that left me unable to contact anyway, and I scarce had time to dress my wounds between battles. Only once in my first ten years of service did I come anywhere near Earth, and I immediately took leave and went there when that happened." He turned his hand and glanced at the balus stone. "I went to tell you that my service was nearly over. That I would then be free to do anything, to go anywhere...to go to *you*."

"But you didn't."

"Because you had already chosen another."

Tears filled her eyes. "And I didn't love him as I loved you! If you had come to me, or just had my father call me, you would have known that!"

His eyes gleamed with his own gathering tears. "All I ever had was you, Kiara. If I had gone to see you anyway, if I had seen you with *him* and learned, without a doubt, that you were happy, that you were whole...what would I have had left?"

Kiara clenched her hands at her sides. "What do you have now?"

He swallowed, holding her gaze. "Nothing."

"I waited, Volcair. I had no idea what you were doing, or what duties you were fulfilling, or whether you were alive or dead. I deserved to know. I deserved some word from you, something. Anything." Tears spilled down her cheeks, and her throat tightened upon her next words. "You were a coward. That's what you chose."

Volcair flinched. With hurt and confusion contorting his face, he extended an arm toward her. "Kiara, I fought across the universe with no thoughts but of getting back to you."

She jerked back out of his reach. "But you didn't fight *for* me, did you? When it came to that battle, you just gave up and ran away."

His expression hardened, and he curled his extended hand into a loose fist before dropping it. "I fought for you today. And I will forever after."

Kiara shook her head. "No. You can't stand there after calling me unfaithful and act like you're all for me now. You saved my life and the lives of my crew today, and I'll always be thankful for that, but...but you were just fulfilling your duty as commander. That's all it was."

"Kiara, I would not have—"

She pointed to the door. "I want you to leave."

He kept his expression surprisingly composed, but the pain in his eyes nearly undid her. Cypher whined. Kiara refused to look at the inux; seeing his sadness would be enough to break her.

"If you require anything, any of my officers would be glad to assist," Volcair said in a soft voice before he turned and exited the room.

As soon as the door closed, Kiara dropped to her knees and pressed her lips together, holding back an agonized cry until it was too strong to contain. She fell forward, burying her face in her folded arms as she lay on the floor. Her body shook with wrenching sobs. Emptiness spread through her, originating in her chest.

This felt like losing him all over again, like her heart had been ripped out of her chest, leaving a vast, painful hollow behind.

There was a thump on the floor, and a second later, Cypher nudged her elbow with his snout. Kiara lifted her arm, and he nestled beneath it. His nose brushed against her moistened cheek.

"He came back, Cypher," she rasped. "H-He came back, and I never knew."

Cypher warbled and whined again but remained by her side—just as he had for all these years.

If only she'd had Volcair at her side, too.

EIGHT

Volcair stepped into his quarters, closed the door, and stood in silence. The necklace dangling from his clenched fist felt impossibly heavy—as heavy as his unfulfilled promise.

I will find my way back.

He'd returned to Earth seven years ago, but he'd never gone back to *Kiara*. He'd failed her. And his thoughtless, harsh words a few minutes ago had only torn open the old wounds his absence had left on her heart.

Though his emotions were so volatile and tumultuous that they made him physically ill, he refused to sit. He stalked forward, spun on his heel when he neared the far wall, and walked back toward the door only to start the circuit again. His pacing did nothing to settle his mood, but it offered an outlet for the restless, anxious energy coursing through him.

Just one more time, he'd told himself, *just one more glimpse of her, just to see that she is safe and happy.* But he'd known he would never be satisfied; he'd never get enough of her. He would always yearn for more.

I had that last glimpse. And now I know I'm the one who

smashed whatever happiness she might've had—not just for today, but for all the years that have separated us.

It had been neither the reunion he'd imagined nor the reunion he'd hoped for. He wanted Kiara more than he wanted anything else in the universe, but the thought of her compromising who she was—who he *knew* her to be despite their years apart—had crushed him inside. She'd never been one to conform to tradition, not even the traditions of her own people, but she'd always been honest, kind, and faithful.

He would never have asked her to betray her mate for him. The thought that she'd done so had hit Volcair so hard, so fast, that he'd exploded. Nearly two decades of frustration, bitterness, and loneliness had roiled inside him, and he'd directed it all at her.

He'd hurt her, despite the long ago vow he'd made to himself to never do her harm.

I eventually break all my promises.

What he'd done had been a worse betrayal than he'd accused her of committing.

"She was right," he whispered. "I am a coward."

He'd faced armed foes, supposedly impenetrable fortifications, impossibly large hostile fleets, but he had been unable to face her when it mattered most. He had been unable to face the chance of being hurt, unable to face potential rejection.

So he'd fled. He'd fled Earth, and he'd fled her, too afraid to know whether she would choose him when given the choice.

When it mattered most, he had failed to fight for her. Today could not make up for that. He could spend his entire life trying to atone, and it would never be enough. She'd waited, and he'd given up. He could not blame her for moving on after so long without word from him. Years of battle and constant redeployment across the farthest reaches of Dominion space were no excuse. He could have found a way to contact her, to tell her he would come as soon as he could.

To tell her to keep hoping.

To keep waiting.

Volcair halted and lifted his hand, staring down at the balus stone as it fell against the inside of his wrist.

But she kept this. She broke off her engagement and kept this.

He tightened his grip on the chain.

She was still waiting for me.

That was so much more than he'd had any right to expect. They were only teenagers when he'd left Earth; what had either of them truly known about relationships? They'd been apart now for more than half their lives. She'd had no obligation to wait; the burden he'd placed upon Kiara by asking her to had been unfair.

He was the one who'd been obligated by his promises, and he'd been the one who failed to act upon them. He hadn't even tried to fight for her.

And I didn't love him as I loved you!

Had he pushed past his own fear, he would've learned that seven years ago. He would never have committed to a five-year extension to his military service and could instead have spent the last five years with *her*, devoted to *her*.

Loving her.

It wasn't too late; it *couldn't* be. After all this time, their paths had crossed, and a situation had arisen that entwined their lives once again. He wasn't sure if that meant anything—if it was part of fate's machinations—but it could. It could mean something if he worked to give it meaning.

After nineteen years of separation, the female he'd recognized as his mate was nearby—only a few doors down the hall.

A few meters separated them now, rather than countless light years, but somehow the distance felt just as vast.

He dropped his hand, opening his fingers to catch the balus stone in his palm before closing his fist.

The distance should never have stopped him before, and he would not let it stop him now. All he had to do was convince Kiara to talk with him—while dealing with the aftermath of the hijacking and keeping a city-sized space station operating normally.

Oddly, it was the first task that seemed the most daunting—but which also promised the greatest reward.

Once he'd composed himself, he placed the necklace in his pocket and returned to duty, spending the rest of his day—and part of his night, which he'd always found difficult to gauge due to the lack of day-night cycles on space stations—in his office, dealing with reports, inspections, and the logistics of launching a search for the pirates who'd attacked the *Starlight*. All the pirates on Kiara's ship had fought to the death, but Volcair knew they'd just been a small piece of the group that had carried out the hijacking.

Officers and soldiers came and went throughout that time, delivering information and receiving orders. Due to the immensity of the search area, they were unlikely to locate Vrykhan—even knowing he'd eventually be going to Caldorius—but Volcair wouldn't let that stop the search. The tretin and his pirate fleet had been a scourge on the Dominion's fringes for years.

While Volcair was otherwise occupied, Lieutenant Beltheri stepped up to assist with Janus Six's normal operations, performing with competence and efficiency despite being clearly flustered on several occasions. Volcair was grateful for her performance and professionalism.

Volcair spent every spare moment thinking about Kiara. When he watched the recorded interviews his senior officers had conducted with her crew, he took the longest on hers, often rewinding to earlier points on the recording because he'd lapsed into thought while staring into her eyes and had missed her reply to the interviewer. She looked...sorrowful.

And that was Volcair's fault.

Despite his exhaustion by the time he finally went to bed, Volcair lay awake for a long while. Kiara and her crew had returned to their temporary quarters for rest, and most of his first shift officers were sleeping after working extended hours. There had been a few smugglers caught in the station during his short tenure as commander, and his ships had engaged with pirate vessels out in space more than once, but there'd been nothing quite like the events surrounding the *Starlight*.

It should have been military and administrative matters keeping him awake. Central command would demand regular reports, and Volcair would have to draft a formal request for additional soldiers and ships in the area. He'd also have to navigate the clerical issues around having military personnel perform repairs on a civilian vessel and organize his teams to conduct as thorough and efficient a search as possible. But none of it crossed his mind.

All he could think of was Kiara. He held the necklace between forefinger and thumb as he stared at the dark ceiling, brushing the pad of his thumb along the intricately patterned metal holding the glowing blue stone in place.

Had anything gone differently—had the ship not been registered under Kiara's name, or the borian pirate acted a little more naturally—the *Starlight* would've been released, and its crew would have been sold as slaves on Caldorius. From there, they'd have been sent to any number of worlds where slaves, especially exotic ones like the terrans, were legal.

Even Arthos, the Infinite City—the pinnacle of technology and civilization in the known universe—had an issue with slaves. Slavery wasn't legal there, but it was often overlooked by the authorities due to the difficulty of fighting a problem that originated on countless worlds beyond the Consortium's jurisdiction.

The thought of Kiara suffering such a fate made Volcair's heart ache and his stomach sink even as it sparked an angry fire in his chest—a fire that, ultimately, would have accounted for nothing. He was one person; all his passion and rage would never have been enough to find her, had she been taken. He would have spent the rest of his life searching.

No, that wasn't correct. If she *had* been taken, he would never have known. That only made the *what-ifs* worse; if the ship hadn't been flagged, if he hadn't seen her name on the manifest, he would never have gone to the docking bay. He would never have fought his way into the cargo hold to rescue her from the pirates. He would never have known her ship had passed through his station.

He would never have known she was in any danger.

A soft scratch at the door pulled Volcair from his thoughts. Furrowing his brow, he lifted his head off his pillow and looked toward the door, which was reduced to a rectangular patch of darkness amidst the shadows.

The scratching came again, this time a little more insistent.

Volcair closed his fingers around the necklace, tossed aside the covers, slipped out of bed, and padded to the dresser to pull on a pair of underpants. It wasn't unusual for his subordinates to wake him because some pressing situation had arisen, but they usually contacted him through the station's comm systems. He walked to the door and pressed the button to open it.

The doorway was empty—or at least *appeared* so until he lowered his gaze. Cypher sat on the floor just beyond the threshold, staring up at Volcair with four glowing, impossibly sad eyes. The inux's lips parted, revealing his sharp teeth as he whined.

Frowning, Volcair sank into a crouch. He put out his empty hand, and Cypher stepped forward, brushing his cheek against Volcair's palm.

"I really botched this," Volcair said.

Cypher nodded and moved closer still, rubbing his side along Volcair's leg.

The light scrape of those metal scales against Volcair's calf brought back old, happy memories. Memories of the best years of his life, which had come and gone so long ago—Cypher bouncing over Volcair's bed, clicking excitedly to wake the boy up in the morning; Volcair and Cypher racing through the halls of various embassies on so many different worlds, often to Father's disapproval; Cypher snuggling against Volcair in the night, fighting back the loneliness and despair that had so often assailed the boy in the dark, replacing it with warmth and companionship.

But his fondest memories of Cypher included Kiara. She'd instilled a new energy in the inux, and the three of them had often laughed and played during Volcair's years on Earth. Little had excited Cypher more than their visits with Kiara.

"I missed you, old friend, more than I can ever express." Volcair ran his hand along Cypher's spine, from the inux's head to his flank. "But I am glad you stayed with her. Glad you did what I could not."

Cypher whined again, catching Volcair's wrist carefully

between his metal jaws and giving him a slight tug. The points of the inux's teeth pressed into Volcair's skin but didn't puncture it.

Volcair shook his head. "She does not want to see me now."

Flattening his ears and narrowing his eyes, Cypher tugged harder, making Volcair sway forward. The inux released his hold after a few moments. He sat down, glared up at Volcair, and growled.

Volcair turned his other hand palm up and opened his fingers to stare down at the necklace. He laughed to himself, the sound utterly devoid of humor. "I'm doing it again. Was I always such a fool?"

Cypher's responding clicks were undoubtedly a *yes*, but the inux softened his honesty by nuzzling Volcair's knee.

"I leave you with her for a little while, and now you're taking her side?" Volcair asked, a soft smile touching his lips. "No more shielding myself behind *duty*. Let's go, Cyph."

Lips drawn back in what could only be a smile, Cypher leapt to his feet and bounded down the corridor toward Kiara's room.

Unmindful of his state of dress, Volcair rose and followed Cypher. His heart thumped, and all his fears, insecurities, and inadequacies seemed to bubble to the surface at once, threatening to paralyze him. But he would not stop now. He would see this through to the end, however long it took, however hard he had to fight.

Kiara would be his.

Kiara *was* his.

The door to her room was closed. Volcair stopped in front of it and glanced down at Cypher, who lifted his front paws and scratched at the metal.

Sounds of movement came from the other side of the

door, and it slid open a moment later, revealing a tired-eyed Kiara. Her mass of curls was held up by a colorful, patterned scarf, and she wore little more than a scrap of black underwear and a white tank top through which her dark nipples were visible.

"Cypher, how the bloody hell did you—" Her eyes caught Volcair's and rounded.

That old heat ignited in his chest and coursed through his *qal*; he'd always experienced the sensation when he was in her presence, but it was more intense now than ever. It had grown into an instinctual, bone-deep craving. His cock stirred, hardening in an instant.

He wasn't looking at an adolescent, but a woman—the woman who was meant to be his mate. The woman who was meant to be *his*.

Before she said anything more, Volcair stepped into the room, captured her face between his hands, and pressed his lips to hers. He heard Cypher's lightly clacking steps move away down the hall.

Kiara's eyes widened farther, and she gasped. Taking advantage of her surprise, he slapped the button to close the door, returned his hand to her face, and guided her deeper into the room until her back touched the wall. He pinned her there with his body.

She relaxed and gave in to him, parting her lips with a soft moan. Her hands slid up his sides to settle on his upper back. Volcair deepened the kiss, nipping and sucking at her lips, driven only by hunger and instinct—in this, he had no experience, only a desire that had burned in him for years.

The warmth on his skin became a tingling, and that tingling gradually escalated into an electric hum. Kiara's heat radiated into him, and her smooth, bare legs brushed against his. His cock throbbed. Volcair groaned, pressing his shaft more firmly against her.

Kiara stilled. Sliding her hands between their chests, she pushed, interrupting the kiss but not breaking the contact between their bodies.

"What are you doing, Volcair?" she asked, her quiet voice laced with pain and uncertainty. Her skin glowed with the reflected light of his *qal*.

"You are *mine*, Kiara," he said, tipping his forehead against hers, "and I should've gone to you. I should never have left you."

"But you did leave, and you never came back. All those years gone, and you accused me of—"

"I know," he rasped, "and I will forever hold those words and those wasted years as my greatest regrets. Let me spend what time I have left making up for it. Let me atone for my cowardice. I truly have nothing without you."

He drew back from her, took hold of her hands, and guided them to his chest. He flattened her palms over his *qal*. "Do you remember the first time we met? Do you remember how my *qal* glowed when you touched them?"

Her dark eyes, gleaming with his light, met his. "Yes. They reminded me of starlight."

"They glowed *for you*. I did not understand it then, but I do now. Even as a child, part of me recognized that you are my mate. That you are mine."

She pulled her hands free, and he released his hold on her. With trembling fingers, she lightly traced the *qal* on his chest, following it up and over his shoulders. "But I'm human. How could I be?"

"How doesn't matter," he said in English, "only that you are."

"What about your ancestry, and the purity of your species? I know how much that means to your people."

Volcair shook his head. "You mean more to me than any of that. More to me than them. I was obligated to serve. I volunteered for more time only because I thought I'd already lost you. My people..." He drew in a deep breath and released it slowly; this was a truth his father would never have wanted to hear, a truth that would bring Volcair shame and criticism among his kind. "My people have always been—and will always be—second to you. I never would've left had I been given the choice."

Tears filled her eyes. "But you *did* have the choice to come back, Volcair."

He clenched his jaw and squeezed his eyes shut for a moment. "And I am sorry for it, sorry beyond words. It is no excuse, no justification, but...it would have killed me to see you in the arms of another. To see you happy with another. To see with my own eyes that you had chosen, and that your choice was not me."

"I'm sorry, Volcair," she said, voice tight. "I'm so s—"

He opened his eyes and pressed a thumb over her lips, silencing her. Kiara's tears slid down her cheeks, and he brushed them away. "No. You need never apologize for what you did. *Never*."

Lowering his arms, he took hold of one of her wrists and turned her hand palm up. He settled the necklace on her open palm, allowing the delicate chain to slide off his fingers and pile around the balus stone. "When we were children, you were my best mate. My only mate. Will you be my *forever* mate?"

Though a heavy sob shook her, Kiara smiled and nodded. "Yes. Yes, Volcair." Closing her fingers around the necklace, she threw her arms around him and pressed her face against his neck. "You've always been the only one for me. I knew it even as a child."

Volcair embraced her and settled his cheek atop her hair, relishing the feel of her warm body against his. He thought this closeness had been lost to him, that he'd never experience it again. Joy and relief overwhelmed him; his mate was here, in his arms, after all these years.

His mate.

She shifted to press her lips against his neck, and her hard nipples brushed his chest. The desire he'd felt when she first opened the door came roaring back. His *qal* burned with it, and he curled his fingers, clutching her closer.

Kiara wiggled her hips, rubbing her pelvis against his cock.

Volcair shuddered and groaned. He gritted his teeth and dropped his hands to her waist, stilling her movements. His fingers found the patch of bare skin between the hem of her tank top and the band of her underwear.

In all the years since he'd met Kiara, there had never been another for him. There'd only ever been her on his mind, in his heart, in his dreams, and having her in his arms now, so warm and soft, smelling so delectable, there was no way he could hold himself back.

"Kiara..."

"I want this," she said softly, tilting her head back to meet his gaze. She reached down between them, grasped the bottom of her tank top, and pulled it up over her head, dropping it to the floor at her feet. The necklace fell atop it. "I want you. Now. We've wasted too much time already."

Volcair's heart hammered against his ribs, and his *qal* shone ever brighter as his gaze dipped down her body. Her breasts— each no more than a handful—were tipped with dark, pearled nipples; they were utterly perfect. *She* was utterly perfect.

Kiara hooked the band of her underwear with her thumbs and pushed the black fabric down her legs, baring herself completely. His gaze roamed over her luscious curves, pausing on the small patch of dark hair above her slit.

His breath hitched, and fire blazed through him. This was his mate. His beautiful, tantalizing mate, offering herself to him.

Volcair's eyes locked with hers. He closed the distance between them and placed a hand on the back of Kiara's neck, pulling her close as he slanted his mouth over hers. She returned the kiss with the same fierce urgency he felt in himself. Their lips and tongues caressed each other, exploring and learning; his hunger only grew with each passing moment.

He covered one of her breasts with his hand. Her nipple brushed against his palm before he squeezed, closing his thumb and forefinger around the bud. Kiara moaned and undulated against his groin, causing his hips to buck involuntarily.

She gasped, and they both stilled, staring at each other. Through the thin fabric of his underwear, he felt the damp heat of her arousal nestled against his shaft.

He inhaled, taking in the sweet musk of her desire. His mouth watered, and he experienced a new sort of hunger—one that could only be sated by her taste upon his tongue.

Volcair dropped to his knees, curled his hands around Kiara's thighs, spread her legs, and pressed his mouth to her sex.

Her flavor, ambrosial and pure, swept across his tongue, which he extended for a deeper taste, running it from the bottom of her delicate folds to the top. The tip of his tongue flicked against a hard little nub at the apex of her sex.

Kiara cried out. Her back hit the wall, and he paused, curious. Raising one of her legs over his shoulder, he opened her wider for his inspection. Volcair gazed at her dark petals, which were splayed open to reveal the pink of her inner depths. And there, at the top of her slit, was the small bud he'd discovered with his tongue.

He looked higher; Kiara stared down at him with dark, heavy-lidded eyes. Volcair flicked his tongue against the nub again. She inhaled sharply, and her hips twitched.

"This feels good?" he asked.

"Yes," she whispered.

Unable to deny her—unable to deny *himself*—Volcair lowered his mouth over the nub and sucked.

Kiara moaned and dropped her hands to his head, clutching his hair; the sharp sting on his scalp only added to the exquisite torture and deep, aching need in his cock. Spurred on by his mate's throaty cries, husky pleas, and divine taste, Volcair ravaged her with his mouth and tongue. He couldn't get enough of her sweet nectar.

With a growl, he latched back onto the little bud that brought her so much pleasure. Kiara tensed just before a scream tore from her throat. She rocked against his mouth, and Volcair grasped her hips, shoving them firmly against the wall as he speared her tight, quivering channel with his tongue, drinking the nectar she gifted him.

When her trembling eased, Volcair turned his face and kissed her inner thigh.

"Volcair," she said softly.

Carefully lowering her leg from his shoulder, Volcair tilted his head back to look up at his mate. Her cheeks were flushed, her lips plump, and her lust-hazed eyes were half-lidded. This image of his mate pleasured and bared to him was the most erotic and beautiful sight he'd ever seen.

Were it not for the discipline he'd learned in the military, he would have spilled his seed then and there, before ever joining with her. Even with all his willpower bent toward restraint, his hold on himself was tenuous.

Wrapping his arms around her, Volcair lifted her off the floor. She smiled tenderly and dropped her hands to his shoulders to steady herself as he carried her to the bed.

He gently laid her upon the bedding, his need battering his dwindling self-control as he looked upon her; she parted her thighs to reveal her wet folds.

"Now, Volcair," she said, brushing her foot along the outside of his leg. "Make love to me."

He didn't immediately comply; he stared at her, locking this moment in his mind, enshrining every detail in his memory, emblazoning Kiara in his heart. He wanted to hold onto this image forever—his mate, the most beautiful creature in all the universe, waiting for him with desire gleaming in her dark eyes.

Volcair dropped his hands to the waistband of his underpants and forced them down. He kicked them aside once they fell around his ankles. Without removing his eyes from Kiara, he climbed onto the bed and crawled over her. She spread her legs wider, cradling his hips between her thighs.

Kiara placed a hand on his chest and slid it down; a moment later, she curled her fingers around his cock. The pressure within him rocketed nearly to the breaking point, sending a shudder through his entire body before his muscles stiffened. He hissed through his teeth and placed his hand over hers.

My mate is as bold as ever.

"Kiara, I will not last," Volcair grated.

Her fingers moved beneath his, tracing the sensitive nodules lining his shaft. "You're...different."

Each brush of a fingertip over those bumps stole a little more of his breath and pushed him closer to the edge. The pleasure her touch caused was so powerful, so overwhelming, that he could not make sense of her words. "Different?"

"Different," she repeated, her lips curving into a smile. "A *good* different."

Though her smile eased any insecurity he might have felt, understanding continued to elude him. All he wanted was to please her, to give her what *she* wanted, despite his own need reaching previously unimaginable levels. "Different how?"

Chuckling, Kiara lifted her head and kissed his jaw. She tightened her grip on his shaft and stroked it. "Well, you're not human."

Volcair grunted, clutching the bedding in his fists.

She teased one of the nodules with the tip of her finger. "These little bumps here? They're going to hit *all* the right places inside me."

His eyelids fluttered shut; he was utterly at her mercy, a slave to her slightest touch. "I have never done this," he said between ragged breaths. "Never joined with anyone."

The motion of her hand stilled, and it fell away from his cock. He nearly begged for her to put it back. He opened his eyes to look down at her. She lay with lips parted, eyes rounded, her expression laced with shock and guilt.

"You never... Even knowing that I..." Her chest rose and fell with short, shallow breaths, and tears glimmered in her eyes.

Volcair lowered himself onto his elbows, settling his hips between her thighs. With one hand, he cupped her face, making sure her eyes remained on his. His cock throbbed and ached, desperate for release, but that didn't matter. She was what mattered.

"Kiara, why are you crying?" he asked softly.

"You n-never gave up. Not like I—"

Volcair pressed his mouth to hers, silencing her. When he

pulled back, he said, "This is *now*, Kiara, and we are both here. We will only go forward. *Together*."

She nodded and slipped her fingers into his hair. "Together."

He brushed his thumb across her cheek and smiled. "My lovely mate." He lowered his mouth and kissed her as he adjusted his hips to press the head of his cock against the entrance of her sex. "My Kiara."

Volcair rolled his hips forward, and his shaft sank into her slick, welcoming heat. Kiara echoed his groan and spread her thighs farther. He pulled back only to press into her harder, deeper, thrusting until his pelvis touched hers. Her inner walls tightened around him, drawing him in.

Releasing a shuddering breath, he stilled, propping himself over her as he fought to contain the pressure, as he fought to hold himself together; he knew it would always be a losing battle when it came to her, but he planned to relish every moment of it.

KIARA'S BREATH hitched as Volcair thrust into her; he stretched her, and his nodules rubbed her clit and inner walls with every stroke of his shaft. Pleasure rippled through her, producing a fresh wave of liquid heat between her legs.

She stared up at him, unable to look away from his entrancing, glowing eyes. Her heart was full to bursting. It was difficult to breathe, difficult to form coherent words, difficult to *think* with the torrent of emotions sweeping through her. This was Volcair, the man she'd waited a lifetime for. The man she loved with all her being.

Wrapping her legs around him, she undulated her hips to match his rhythm, taking him deeper and deeper, her need growing and growing. She wanted all of him, everything he had to give. Tilting her head back, Kiara released a throaty sigh, but kept her gaze locked with his.

Volcair bared his teeth and quickened his pace. The definition of his sculpted muscles was enhanced by the light from his *qal*, which brightened with each of his motions. He said her name; it was barely a whisper, but it flowed from his lips like a prayer, like a plea.

Her core clenched, and delightful shivers skated across the surface of her skin. She clutched his hair as the sensation grew in intensity with Volcair's every thrust. The bumps along his shaft added to the friction, making the pressure in her build with blistering, impossible speed; too quickly, he catapulted her into blissful oblivion.

"Volcair," she breathed, catching her bottom lip between her teeth as her inner walls convulsed. She cried out as pleasure crashed through her, tensing her muscles, leaving her helpless but to succumb to the onslaught. It was only then that she allowed her eyes to close. Volcair became her entire world—his smooth skin, his shaft filling her, his hard muscles, the warmth of his breath, his scent mingling with her own.

The sound of his voice filled her ears as he released a ragged, wordless cry. His body shuddered around Kiara, *within* her, his cock swelling as his heat flooded her. His movements became erratic, rough, and desperate, only heightening her rapture.

Though tremors continued to course through her body, Kiara forced her eyes open and looked upon Volcair while he was in the throes of ecstasy. His head was thrown back, his eyes squeezed shut, and his *qal* shone brighter than she'd ever seen. He was beautiful.

And he was *hers*.

Volcair sagged forward, catching himself with his elbows to either side of Kiara as he let out a long, heavy breath. His pecs pressed down on her breasts, brushing against her hardened nipples. He opened his eyes and met her gaze.

"Kiara," he said, voice husky. His lips remained parted as though he meant to say more while he searched her face, but he said it all by lowering his mouth over hers for another searing, claiming kiss.

She returned the kiss, giving over to that claim.

For the first time in so long, she felt like she was exactly where she was meant to be. Everything in her life had led up to this moment—including the heartache and loneliness. Everything had led her here, to *him*, so she could finally be whole. Volcair had always been the missing piece of her heart, and she'd finally fit that piece into place.

Tears stung her eyes. "I love you, Volcair. My star. I've always loved you."

His features softened, and he shifted his weight onto one elbow so he could settle his hand on her cheek. "And I have always loved you, Kiara. I am sorry it has taken me so long to act upon it."

Kiara lifted her head and pressed her lips against his. "We won't look back."

He smiled. "Only forward."

NINE

Kiara slowly stirred from her dreams—her wonderful, blissful dreams.

A lazy smile spread across her lips, and her naked limbs glided over the cool sheets as she stretched. Images of the night before flashed through her mind—caressing lips, exploring hands, entwined bodies.

Kiara stilled. Her heart leapt as she opened her eyes and raised her head, scanning the room.

She was alone.

Had it all been a vivid dream? Had she simply longed for Volcair so badly that her subconscious had taken over, making her mind and body believe everything she'd dreamt had been real?

No.

He'd been with her. He'd made *love* to her. She could still smell him around her, in the sheets, on her skin. He was everywhere. There was a heaviness in her core, and her thighs were sticky with his seed.

She caught her lower lip between her teeth as she smiled.

They'd made love three times before finally succumbing to sleep in each other's arms.

Though she longed to feel his warmth again, she shouldn't have been surprised by his absence. He was the commander of this space station. He had duties to attend to. She couldn't—and didn't—expect him to abandon those duties now. She knew he was still nearby, waiting for her.

Gathering the bedding, she brought it to her nose and inhaled deeply, drawing in his crisp, spicy scent. She moaned. How could a man smell so *good*?

A metallic glitter caught her eye. She turned her head to the second pillow—the pillow he'd rested his head upon—to find her balus stone necklace resting atop it. Smile widening, she sat up and gathered the necklace, cradling it within her palm to trace its intricate pattern with her fingertip.

Something scratched at the door.

"Give me a few minutes, Cypher," she called.

Kiara tossed the bedding aside and slipped out of bed. She paused, moaning at the sensation between her legs. She was a little sore, but the insistent, aching throb there spoke more of continued need than discomfort. She squeezed her thighs together; it didn't ease her longing.

After setting her necklace on the desk, she hurried to the loo to pee before cleaning up in the bathroom. Once she'd washed, brushed her teeth, and tamed her frizzy curls, she strode back into the room and quickly dressed.

Cypher's scratching had become impatient. He could reach the outside entry button, but it had been temporarily programmed to open only to her—once the inux left the room, he was stuck without her help.

Kiara pressed the interior button, and Cypher leapt inside as soon as the door was wide enough to fit through. He clicked excitedly as he stood on his hind legs and settled his paws on her thighs. He stared up at her with ears perked, teeth bared in a vulpine smile, and tail flicking rapidly behind him.

Grinning, Kiara ran her hand down the back of his neck. "Have you seen Volcair?"

Cypher nodded.

"By your mood, I take it you know everything is good between us?"

He leapt away from her and spun in a circle, grinning wider than ever.

"Could you take me to him?"

With an affirmative warble, he turned and walked through the open doorway.

Kiara followed him into the corridor, pausing briefly to close the door behind her. She'd only made it a few meters when Tekel and Mason turned the nearby corner. They were in the middle of a conversation, but the moment they saw her, they stopped and smiled.

"Hey," Kiara said; her grin felt so big that she wondered if the corners of her mouth were touching her ears.

"I can't believe Kiara—*our* Kiara—is only just getting out of bed," Mason said, crossing his arms. "Do you have any idea what time it is?"

Kiara cleared her throat, her cheeks warming. "Uh...no?"

Mason smirked. "You've never been one to sleep in. Ever."

Tekel snorted, his tail lazily flicking from side to side. "You would know why she slept in, Captain, if your quarters were closer to hers. You would've *heard* why."

Mason glanced at Tekel. "Huh?"

Kiara covered her face with a hand. "I can't believe this."

"Wait, you mean Kiara actually... That she? With *who*?"

Mason looked back and forth between Kiara and Tekel, finally settling his gaze on the azhera. "*You?*"

"No!" Tekel and Kiara cried in unison.

Mason took a step back, holding his hands up, palms out. "Okay, damn. Don't need to yell." He grinned at Kiara. "So... who was it?"

She rolled her eyes. "You're a bigger gossip than my grandmother."

Tekel snickered.

"Come on, Kiara!" Mason said. "I've worked with you for years, and not once—not *once*—have I seen you take any interest in anyone."

"It's...the commander."

Mason's eyes widened and his mouth gaped. "Wait, what? You go from no one for *years* to sleeping with the commander of a space station the same day you met him? And here I thought *I* moved quick."

She couldn't help but laugh. "You're the reason I added the *no sleeping with coworkers* clause to the employment contracts, Mason. But it's...not that simple. Commander Volcair and I have a past. We've known each other since we were little kids."

"Oh. Is that why you chose this route?"

Kiara shook her head. "No. I had no idea he was in charge here. We...lost touch for a long time in between. This was just chance."

"Fate," Tekel said.

Kiara smiled. "You could say that."

Mason grinned and wagged his eyebrows. "So, was he any—"

"Mason, I am not going to discuss what I do in private. And as far as you are concerned, Volcair is *mine*."

Mason laughed. "Okay, okay. I'll only look."

Tekel folded his muscled arms over his wide chest. "Based on the screaming, I'd say he did *very* well."

Heat flooded Kiara's face, but she couldn't deny it—Volcair *had* done very well.

"How's the *Starlight*?" she asked, desperate for a change of subject even though she knew it wouldn't last long.

"Peyton is working with the station's mechanics to assess the damage," Tekel said. "Seems minor, but there may have been a couple hull breaches that need to be repaired."

Kiara nodded. "Good. Mason, I need you to get in touch with our brokers on Deduin, let them know we ran into an emergency and we're delayed for at least a few days. We need to make sure our buyers are aware their cargo is safe."

"Will do," Mason said.

"Now if you'll excuse me, there is someone I need to find."

Mason affectionately patted her back as she and Cypher stepped past him. "Go find your man."

Nope. I'll never hear the end of it.

"See you both later," Kiara called over her shoulder.

Cypher led her through the space station's labyrinthine corridors. She understood all the signs—Volcair had taught her how to read Volturian when she was young, and that knowledge had come in handy in her adult life—but they provided little assistance in navigation; without Cypher, she would've been hopelessly lost after a few minutes.

Several of the uniformed Entris Dominion soldiers, all of whom were volturians descended of different *qalarin*, stared at her curiously as she passed, but she shrugged off their stares and offered friendly smiles in return. The Dominion was massive, and many volturians had never seen a human with their own eyes despite more than two decades of friendship between the UTF and the Dominion.

Finally, they entered a long hallway that was marked *COMMAND* in flowing Volturian letters at its entrance. Most of the soldiers' uniforms here were a little different, a little more refined and elegant—just like Volcair's. She assumed that meant most of them were officers.

No one questioned her as she followed Cypher to an open door at the end of the corridor. She stepped into a large office with bay windows along one wall that overlooked a massive hangar. There were several chairs and a wide, sleek desk arranged within; Volcair was seated at the desk with a female volturian officer standing behind him, looking over his shoulder at a projected screen.

Excitement and anxiousness swept through her as she looked upon Volcair. It was a strange but familiar feeling, one that she'd almost forgotten over the years. With his head bowed over his work, he reminded her of his younger self, bent over her tablet in concentration as he drew something special just for her. In that instant, her mind fully bridged the boy she'd known to the man he'd become.

Cypher clicked, announcing their arrival.

Volcair lifted his head. His eyes met Kiara's, and his lips curled into a smile. Though his face had matured and hardened, his smile was the same as it had always been—and she still couldn't help but feel like his smile, this smile, was *only* for her.

"Sorry," she said. "I can find your later if you're busy."

"No, it is fine," he said. "I had planned to wake you soon. Some of your crew seemed mystified that you were still asleep."

Kiara's skin heated again, and she glanced at the female officer. "I don't make a habit of sleeping in."

Volcair's cheeks darkened slightly—so slightly that she couldn't be entirely sure it had happened—before he turned his head to the female officer. "Lieutenant Beltheri, this is my mate, Kiara Moore. The owner of the *Starlight*."

Surprise flitted across Lieutenant Beltheri's face.

Kiara was surprised herself—he hadn't hesitated to introduce her as his mate. She could tell the woman had questions based on the way her eyes jumped between Kiara and Volcair, but Beltheri didn't voice them.

Instead, the lieutenant offered Kiara a smile and bowed her head. "It is an honor to meet you, Kiara Moore."

"And you, Lieutenant Beltheri," Kiara said, returning the bow.

"Lieutenant, if you would give us a few minutes?" Volcair asked. "Kiara and I have a few matters to discuss."

"Of course, Commander," Beltheri said. She stepped away from the desk and approached the door, nodding to Kiara on her way out. She closed the door behind her.

Once they were alone, Kiara faced Volcair and smiled. "And just what matters would you like to discuss with me?"

He stood up, and with a few flicks of his fingers, expanded the display on the desk and spun it toward her. After walking around the desk, he opened two electronic documents on the holographic screen—the first written in Volturian and the other in English.

"One's a matter of formality, and the other... Well, it's perhaps a bit presumptuous on my part," he said in English.

Kiara arched a brow and turned her attention to the documents, reading the one written in Volturian. When she was done, she furrowed her brow. "Volcair, are you serious? Resigning your post?"

"I am serious, Kiara," he replied as he sat on the edge of his desk. "I'm nearing the end of my voluntary service term. I have two months to declare my intent to the Dominion—further military service, or official discharge with all afforded honors. Even before yesterday, I wasn't sure what choice I'd make. My father has always wanted me to seek a governmental position, but...that was never my ambition."

She'd known even when they were children that he never wanted to follow in his father's footsteps. "What is your ambition?"

"You." His smile fell. "And I thought that was lost to me long ago."

"It's not lost anymore," she said softly.

"No. So my choice became suddenly quite easy."

Kiara clenched her hands at her sides to keep from reaching for him, forcing her attention to the English document. She smirked as she perused it. "Is this really what I think it is?"

Volcair dipped his chin in a small nod. "A proposed contract of employment."

"You realize that, as owner of the company, it is typically up to *me* to offer employment, don't you?"

He shrugged, and his smile returned. "I figured it was worth a shot. I'm going to be out of work in a few months' time."

"And what position are you seeking?"

"Hmm...how does Head of Security sound?"

Kiara stepped in front of him and slipped her arms around his neck. He settled his hands on her hips. She searched his face, her gaze tracing his *qal*, his lips, his cheekbones, until finally stopping on his eyes. Her heart quickened at the heat burning within their white-blue depths.

"I also have a *no sleeping with coworkers* clause in my standard employment contracts," she said. "It wouldn't look good for me to break my own rule."

"I suppose I could found my own company and work for you as a contractor so you don't have to break your rule."

Her smile softened. "Are we moving too fast, Volcair?"

"I think we can move at whatever speed feels right," he replied. "Besides, I have to stay here for a couple more months to complete my obligations, and you have a business to keep in operation. We can't move particularly fast, given that."

The reminder that she would have to leave soon while he remained here was like a blade plunging into her heart. They'd only just found one another again; did their time together really have to end so soon? What if something happened before they were reunited? What if she lost him again?

Volcair lifted one of his hands and settled his palm over her cheek, brushing the pad of his thumb across her cheekbone. "I will not allow anything to keep us apart again, Kiara. Not even me."

Kiara covered his hand with her own and closed her eyes. "We've been apart for almost twenty years, yet a few more months feels unbearable."

"I can't keep you in the officers' quarters for months, Kiara. My superiors would deem it inappropriate, an abuse of my command...but there are civilian lodgings on the station. You can stay there during my remaining service, if you wish to."

Kiara opened her eyes and looked at Volcair. As much as she wanted to say yes, she couldn't. After what her crew had gone through, she *needed* to be there for them, needed to know they were safe. "I can't."

He frowned and nodded, and his voice was soft when he said, "I understand."

Kiara reached out and cupped his face. "I want to stay, Volcair, I want to stay *so* badly, but I—

"You have a duty to fulfill to your crew. I *do* understand, Kiara. And I love you even more for it."

Tears blurred her vision. "You really want me to be your mate?"

"You always were."

She laughed. "I mean, officially, before my people and yours."

"Yes. I want to be your"—he averted his gaze and pressed his lips together for a moment—"your *husband*. That's the word, isn't it?"

Kiara nodded, twining her fingers in his hair. "And I want to be your wife."

Volcair grinned and slid his hands down and to cup her ass, pulling her against him. "We have many years to make up for."

Kiara brushed her lips over his. "Many, many years."

Cypher clicked loudly, startling them. Kiara looked at the inux, who appeared to be a bit put off that they'd forgotten he was in the room.

"Sorry, Cypher," she said, laughing softly.

He made a whirring sound and thumped his tail on the floor.

"You have had her to yourself all this time," Volcair said. "Now you have to share."

Cypher snorted, turned away from them, and strutted to the door. He rose on his hind legs and raised one of his front paws. His scales rippled as he extended his leg to press the button on the wall. The door slid open. Once his paw reverted to its previous shape, he dropped down on all fours, gave Kiara and Volcair one last parting look with snout upturned, and stepped out.

"I guess he doesn't want to share," Volcair said with a chuckle, turning his attention back to Kiara. "We have at least a few more days together here. There's a small military convoy that'll be stopping at the station in a few days, and their commander has agreed to allow any civilian vessels that intend to continue into Dominion space to accompany his ships for protection. I ask that you wait for them, so I know you're protected until you're in safer territory. I can't lose you again."

"We'll wait for them. I can't imagine Vrykhan will be happy once he discovers his *unique merchandise* escaped."

Volcair's fingers flexed, and he pulled her even closer. "As much as it pains me to empathize with scum like that...I understand the sense of loss."

Kiara drew back one of her hands and traced her fingers along the markings on the side of his face. They glowed beneath her touch. "When your service is over, I'll be waiting for you, and we'll make it official. Then you'll *never* be rid of me."

He turned his face to kiss her palm. "It's you who'll never be rid of me, Kiara. You've had me wrapped around your finger since we were children, and I'm wound far too tight to ever go anywhere."

TEN

THE AUTOMATED taxi's door opened, immediately filling the cab with the scent and sound of nighttime rain. After months spent in space, breathing in dry, filtered air, that smell was a welcome change. It was an assurance that she was finally home—but there was still one thing missing.

Kiara grabbed her bag off the seat beside her and slipped out of the taxi. Cypher jumped out onto the sidewalk beside her. The rain was cold, but she stood in the lamplight for few moments, in no hurry to reach her front door. There was so many things that could be taken for granted, and this was one of them.

She loved the rain. As a child, she'd played in the rain every chance she got—to her parents' displeasure—stomping in every puddle, spinning and dancing in the downpour with her tongue stuck out to catch as many drops as she could. Kiara remembered the first time she'd dragged Volcair out into it when they were young.

Their fathers had been in the bollocks room, chatting about some negotiation over drinks, when the rain started. Kiara had snuck Volcair out right past Isaiah and Vantricar—through the front door, totally unnoticed. Volcair had been startled at first, and his entire body had shivered with the chill, yet his eyes had lit up in delight when he'd held his hand out to watch the droplets splash on his palm. She understood even then that he'd missed out on so many childhood experiences that seemed completely natural to her. They'd both been soaked to the bone by the time their fathers had discovered them and demanded they come inside.

Kiara breathed deep as a smile curled on her lips.

Volcair.

He was coming back. Soon. She only needed to wait a little longer before she could touch him, hold him, and kiss him once more. That brief time on Janus Six hadn't been enough, and these past three months without him near had been torturous—for the both of them. They'd been able to communicate through holo calls while she was still in Entris Dominion space, finishing her delivery with the *Starlight*, but once she'd exited Dominion territory for the home trip, that contact had become minimal. She missed the sound his voice. Missed *him*.

Soon, Kiara. You went years without him by your side, what's another couple of months?

"Too bloody long," she muttered, closing the taxi door behind her. The cab pulled away from the curb and drove off.

Chirruping called Kiara's attention down to Cypher. He cocked his head, and his ears twitched, flicking off droplets of water.

Kiara smiled. "Just wishing Volcair was here, too."

He clicked and bobbed his head in agreement. She hadn't been the only one who'd been away from Volcair for so long.

Kiara turned and stared up at her home. The brick building was warm and familiar by daylight, but those windows—which let in so much brightness while the sun was out—were dark and lonely now. This was home, had been for several years, but it wouldn't start feeling like it until Volcair came and helped her fill it with welcoming light. With his starlight.

She knew Volcair was the reason she'd so often insisted on accompanying her crew on their deliveries. Some part of her, small but insistent, felt like the only way she could be a little closer to Volcair was by being out amongst the stars. She'd always known he was out there, somewhere. Even a centimeter nearer to him was better than her and Cypher staying here alone.

Walking toward the door, she shouldered her bag, lifted her wrist and tapped on her holocom, sending out a call to her parents.

"Kiara!" her mother said after the second chime.

"Sorry for calling so late. I just wanted to let you know that I'm home."

"No need to apologize. We're so glad you're back."

"You were gone longer than usual," Isaiah said, a hint of concern in his voice.

Kiara stopped in front of the door, opened her bag, and dug around for her keys. "Yeah, about that... The crew and I kind of ran into a little...trouble."

"What kind of trouble?" Jada asked.

Kiara cringed. She could just imagine the worried expression that was likely on her mother's face. Jada had never been happy that Kiara insisted on traveling with her cargo so often. Even though the Entris Dominion, where she took the majority of her trade, was allied with the UTF, there was a vast amount of space to cross to get there. Anything could happen in that distance—as this last trip had proved.

"You're not allowed to freak out," Kiara said when her knuckles brushed against the cool metal of her keys. She closed her fingers around them and pulled them out.

"I don't like the sound of that. You can't tell your parents not to worry. We're allowed to freak out as much as we like when it comes to our child," Jada said.

"Then let's forget I said anything." Kiara stuck the key into the lock and turned it, pushing the door open and stepping inside. "The trip was wonderful, and the crew is doing great. Oh! Tekel and Mason really loved the biscuits you sent them, and—"

"Kiara..." Isaiah intoned.

Kiara groaned and glanced at Cypher as he padded through the doorway, his metal scales rippling to shed the water from his body. He looked back at her, jaw parted with his sharp teeth bared in what could only be a mocking grin that said, *You're in for it now.*

She sighed, shut her door, locked it, and tossed her keys on the table nearby. "Pirates."

For the next several minutes, she told her parents the entire story, cringing at each of their responses—all of which held a blend of concern, horror, and anger. At one point, Cypher huffed with laughter as he swaggered past her, leapt onto the sofa, curled up, and laid down. All four of his eyes glinted with amusement.

She glared at him, but her smirk was proof that she wasn't really annoyed with him.

Kiara understood her parents' worry—and she knew they understood that she wouldn't be persuaded to give up the work she was doing. She wasn't going to send her employees, several of whom had become close friends, out there without being willing to take the same risks they were.

Of course, knowing that Kiara wouldn't be dissuaded had never stopped her mother and father from trying.

"But everything is fine," Kiara said as she made her way upstairs. "I'm fine, the crew is fine. No one was seriously hurt. Dominion soldiers boarded the ship and took down the pirates with Cypher's help. Well, mainly one soldier, the commander." She stopped at the top, her hand tightening on the banister. "Volcair Vantricar."

Silence followed. It was her father who first broke it.

"Kiara—"

"Why didn't you tell me Volcair came back?" Kiara asked, eyes stinging with sudden tears.

Silence again. She couldn't imagine what was going through her parents' minds in those moments, but knew it couldn't overcome her hurt.

"After so many years of seeing your joy fade, of seeing you unhappy, you were finally yourself again," Isaiah finally said, his voice raw. "You were with Daniel. You were moving forward in life after standing still for so long."

"You knew how much Volcair meant to me. Had I known he'd come back..." Kiara brushed the tear of her cheek as it spilled from her eye. "I never loved Daniel. Even when I was with him, I was still in love with Volcair. You should have *told* me."

"I should have, Kiara, but... I didn't know. If you weren't happy with Daniel, you never showed it, and you never said anything to us. We've never wanted anything more than for you to be safe and happy. I...I wanted to prevent you from being hurt more than you already had."

Kiara moved down the dark hall toward her bedroom, opened the door, and flicked on the lights. She couldn't prevent the sniffle as she entered the room, walked to the bed, and dropped her bag atop it.

"We didn't keep it from you to hurt you," Jada said softly.

"I know," Kiara said. "And I...I understand. I'm not going to lie and say it doesn't hurt, because it *really* does, and had I known, it would have changed *so* much. But what's done is done. And now...I have a way for you to both make it up to me."

"Anything," Isaiah said.

Kiara grinned, her happiness immediately pushing away any lingering hurt and sadness. She sat on the edge of the bed. "You can help plan my wedding."

"Your wedding?" they both asked.

"I wasn't the only one who couldn't move on. Volcair and I are mates...and really, we have been since we were kids. All that's left is for us to make it official—for the UTF and the Dominion both, if we can."

"You... Volcair and you..." Jada laughed. "Even after all this time?"

"It was fate, Mum."

"You always said that he was yours," Isaiah said with a chuckle.

"You bet your bollocks he is."

"Kiara!" Jada admonished. "Language!"

Kiara laughed.

They talked for a little longer before she told her parents she loved them and said goodnight. She unpacked her bag, tossing the dirty clothing into the laundry basket, set her tablet on her nightstand, and took a quick shower. By the time she finished and pulled on her underwear and a tank top, it was nearly eleven o'clock.

She padded to the bedroom door and leaned out into the hallway. "Goodnight, Cypher!"

An answering chirrup sounded from downstairs.

Smiling, she closed her door and walked to her bed.

Kiara drew back the covers, crawled into bed, and pulled the blankets over her lap. She picked up the tablet. Running her finger over the screen to activate it, she flipped through the commands until she found Volcair's contact number. Longing filled her. The last few times she'd called—the most recent being the moment she'd touched down on Earth—he hadn't answered. He was most likely somewhere out of reach; she knew he'd been traveling lately, finishing up his military service and settling his remaining business within the Dominion. According to the last word she'd had from him, he should've been en route to Arthos now.

Volcair was going to see his father for the first time in a long, long while.

She'd just call him and leave a message telling him that she loved and missed him and wish him a goodnight. Kiara tapped the call icon and stared at the screen as the chiming tone of the outgoing call played.

After the sixth repeat of the tone, the screen changed to display the timer of a connected call. She only expected to hear the generic greeting he'd set for his messenger service.

"Kiara," Volcair said, his voice caressing her name.

Her breath hitched, and she tightened her grip on the tablet. That definitely wasn't the prerecorded greeting she'd heard at least a dozen times over the last few months.

"You're really there?" she asked.

"I'm here."

She squealed and bounced in place. Perhaps she should've been embarrassed by her reaction, but at this moment, she didn't give a bloody damn if her neighbors—or the whole world —heard her. "Switch to visual. I need to see you."

He laughed, and a moment later the tablet's projection flickered again to depict Volcair in a three-dimensional hologram. For a second or two, she could only stare. She'd seen him via holo calls a number of times since leaving Janus Six, and physically he looked exactly the same as he had in person on the space station, but there was a definite difference in him since he'd taken off his uniform for the last time. He seemed... lighter. *Brighter*. His lips were curled up easily in a smile now, and the hint of darkness that had always been in his eyes—even as far back as when they were children—had finally dwindled almost to nothing.

Only his upper body was visible, clad in a form-fitting tunic that matched the dark blue of his shoulder-length hair and accented his toned body. His posture was relaxed; sometimes it seemed like she might've been the only one to have ever seen him in such a state over the course of his entire life. She ran her eyes over his face, and her belly fluttered as it always had when she looked at him. As a boy, he'd always been beautiful, but as a man...

"You *are* going to let me see you, too, right?" he asked.

She chuckled, sure she was wearing the silliest, most love-struck grin in all the universe. Kiara couldn't help it; she hadn't felt this way in years.

She tapped the visual icon on the tablet's screen. His gaze locked with hers, and her heart leapt.

"I didn't expect you to answer," Kiara said. "Where are you?"

"Still traveling to Arthos. A few more hours, and I'll officially be in Consortium space...and I won't be able to talk to you until I leave."

"Then we have some time."

Volcair's smile widened, though it was slightly offset by a gleam of longing in his eyes. "I can't wait until I can say I'll always have time for you and be able to uphold it." He lifted a hand and raked his fingers through his hair, dragging it back behind a pointed ear. "I received your last message just a few minutes ago. Are you home now?"

"I am. All snug and cozy in bed, but quite lonely. Cypher likes to rest downstairs when we're home to guard the door." Kiara leaned back against her pillow, which was propped up against the headboard. "I called you to leave a message saying goodnight, but this is much better."

"It certainly is."

"I spoke to my parents when I got in. I...asked them why they never told me about you coming back."

Volcair frowned, and a little crease formed between his eyebrows. "Is everything all right?"

Kiara nodded. "I was hurt, but I wasn't angry. Everything is fine, though. I didn't want to dwell on the past. I understand why my father did it, and I told them about you, about us." She smiled. "They are happy for us. They've always loved you."

His frown eased, and his expression softened. "I'm glad to hear it. I've always loved your parents, as well. They were very kind to me. And I understand why he didn't tell you, too, as much as I wish things had gone differently."

"What of you?" She frowned. "You're going to see your father for the first time in years. Are you all right?"

Volcair shrugged and shook his head. "I don't know. I haven't really sorted it all out yet. I don't even know what I want to say to him, if I'm being honest. I just... I just need to speak with him before we take this last step."

"Just be honest with him, Volcair. But be understanding,

too. I know he's always been...formal and uptight, but you are his son, and he does care about you."

Volcair's jaw clenched. His shoulders rose as he took in a deep breath and slowly released it, his nostrils flaring as he shifted his gaze to look off to the side somewhere.

"I wish I could be there with you," she said gently.

"We'll be together soon enough, regardless of how this goes." The tension drained from him, and he laughed, shook his head, and returned his attention to her. "How is it that these three months have felt longer than the last nineteen years, even though we've been talking to each other this time?"

"Anticipation, maybe? Because finally, after all this time, we're closer to being together than ever before." She reached out and ran her finger along the image of his cheek. "And we've both had a taste of what we'll have once we're together."

His smile tilted up at one corner wickedly, and the light in his eyes gained a new heat—a heat that matched the sudden glow of his *qal*. "I wish I could have a taste now."

Warmth flooded Kiara and pooled low in her belly. She grinned. "And what is it you would like to taste?"

"Your lips. Your skin." His eyes trailed from hers and moved down. "Your breasts. Your passion. All of you, Kiara. Every last bit."

Her nipples tightened, hardening into achy little buds, and her sex clenched. More than anything she wanted his mouth and tongue on her, licking, sucking, biting, stroking...

A sudden idea came to her mind.

Raising a hand, she lazily brushed the tip of her finger back and forth over the neckline of her tank top and stared at him with her eyes half-lidded. "Volcair? Would you take off your shirt?"

His brows lowered slightly, and his lips parted, allowing

his tongue to slip out for an instant. "It *is* warm in here." He lifted his hands to his shirt and slowly unfastened the buttons. He started at the top and worked his way down, revealing his pale blue flesh—with its shining *qal* marks—a little at a time.

Kiara trailed her eyes over the muscles of his chest and abdomen, her fingers twitching with the need to touch him, to feel his warmth. "If I were there, standing in front of you, I'd unbutton your shirt for you and slide my hands over your chest and shoulders as I removed it."

As he undid the last button, he released a heavy breath and scooted his chair back from the holo recorder, revealing his legs. "I'd place my hands on your hips"—he leaned forward and shrugged his shirt off his shoulders, letting the garment fall onto the chair behind him—"and run them up your sides, lifting your shirt with them."

Sitting up, Kiara kicked the covers off her legs and laid the tablet on the bed in front of her, far enough away that he could see all of her. Keeping her eyes on his, she placed her hands on her sides, caught the hem of her tank top with fingers, and slid her hands up, baring her middle. "Like this?"

"Slower," he breathed, running his hands over his chest. "I want you to feel the fabric rasp over your skin, over your breasts. I want my touch to send a thrill through your body as I bare you to my eyes."

Kiara did as he instructed, pulling her tank top farther up her body, imagining it was his calloused fingers on her skin. Air kissed her nipples. She tossed the tank top aside. "What will do you now?"

Once again, his tongue slipped out and ran across his lips; his *qal* was even brighter than a moment before. She could feel how wet she was, knew her slick was soaking through her underwear. She wanted to trail her tongue over every single one of those marks on his body.

"I'd lean close," he said, voice husky, "just close enough for you to feel the warmth of my breath over your skin. So close, but I wouldn't touch. Not yet. Not until you're begging me for it."

Her breath quickened as tingles skittered across her skin. How was it possible for his words to produce such a powerful reaction, as though she could really feel his breath, warm and teasing, on her skin? Kiara leaned back against the headboard and moaned, arching her back. "Touch me, Volcair."

A groan, low and sexy, resonated from his chest.

"Cup your breasts, Kiara," Volcair said, and hummed when she obeyed. "Caress them. Harder. Yes, like that. Imagine my fingers running over them, my mouth on them, sucking deep. Pinch those sweet nipples, my mate."

Kiara's lips parted in a gasp as she squeezed her nipples, sending a jolt of sensation straight to her core that only deepened her needful ache. Her eyelids drifted shut, and she tilted her head back.

"Open your eyes," Volcair commanded, "and look at me. Do not look away."

She'd never heard him speak so firmly, so unrelentingly, had never experienced him seizing control quite like this. The hard edge in his voice assaulted her with a fresh gush of heat. She opened her eyes and met his. His gaze glowed with the intensity of a thousand stars.

"Feel me, Kiara," he growled. One of his hands was pressed down on his groin, and his chest heaved with ragged breaths. "Do you ache for me?"

"Yes," she breathed, her voice barely making a sound.

"Show me. Take off your panties."

Kiara dropped her hands to her underwear, hooked her thumbs under the waistband, and lifted her backside as she dragged them down, sliding them along her legs. Once they were off, she tossed them over the side of the bed to land somewhere on the floor.

Volcair's eyes remained on her, watching her every move with growing hunger, and her heart pounded as she watched him in turn. He stroked his palm over the bulge of his erection, clearly visible through his pants.

She kept her knees pressed tight in front of her, not allowing him a glimpse of what she knew he longed to see. "Do you ache for me, Volcair?"

He groaned. "Down to my very core."

"Then show *me*. Let me see you."

Volcair tipped his head back, eyelids fluttering, as he squeezed his shaft. He released another heavy breath—one she could almost feel glide across her thighs—and shifted both hands to the waist of his pants. Despite the need burning in his eyes and along his *qal*, he unfastened his belt and pants with agonizing, deliberate slowness.

It only intensified the throbbing between her legs.

Shifting his hips, he pulled his pants open. His cock sprang out, long, thick, and hard, twitching slightly as though with his rapid pulse. Her sex clenched as she remembered the feel of the nodules lining his shaft rubbing her inner walls in all the right spots.

He wrapped his fingers around the base of his shaft and released a hiss through his teeth. "Spread your legs, Kiara. Show me your desire."

Kiara settled back against the pillow and headboard once more and parted her legs. Volcair's eyes dipped and fixated on her sex. His features went taut, and he tightened his hand around his cock, making the muscles in his arm bulge.

"Do you see how wet I am, Volcair?" she asked. "How much I want you, *need* you?

He groaned again; this time the sound was more strained, more prolonged, more desperate. "I can almost taste it."

Kiara nearly closed her eyes at the memory of his tongue between her thighs, but she forced them to remain open. "And I can almost feel it."

"Touch yourself, Kiara."

Her skin prickled at the rough, raspy quality of his voice, and more liquid heat gathered at her core. Laying her hand on her belly, she slowly slid it down over her pelvis, past the small patch of coarse hair above her sex. She dipped her fingers between her folds, grazing her clit, before moving lower to gather and spread her slick. A shiver rippled through Kiara when she returned her finger to her clit, and her breath hitched as she leisurely circled it.

Volcair stroked his fist up and down his length. His nostrils flared, and the intensity in his eyes only increased. "It should be my fingers on your slit. My lips and tongue. Were I with you now, I'd be devouring you, Kiara. You're *mine.*"

Kiara cupped her breast with her other hand and kneaded it, catching her nipple between her finger and thumb to pinch and twist as she continued to work her clit. Whispers of pleasure skittered through her, awakening every nerve ending and setting them ablaze. She caught her bottom lip between her teeth. This felt good, but it was nowhere near as good as his touch had been. Just as she craved his hands on her, she wanted to feel his heat beneath her palms, to replace his hand with her own, to feel his cock throb in her grasp as she pumped her fist up and down. To climb onto his lap and take his length into her body, centimeter by centimeter, until he filled her completely.

A drop of moisture gathered at the tip of his cock, and she avidly watched as he ran his palm over it and stroked his hand back down his shaft. Kiara slid her finger lower toward her center and slipped it into her depths, pumping it in time with his hand.

Volcair growled low. "Tell me you're mine."

"I'm yours, Volcair," she moaned as the pleasure spread through her limbs, pulsing outward from her core. "I've always have been yours."

"And always will be. Faster, Kiara. Deeper." He sped the pace of his hand and bared his teeth. "Feel my touch. Feel *me*."

Kiara added a second finger, pushing them as deep as she could, imagining it was his cock shoving into her. She imagined his body covering hers, caging her in, imagined his heat surrounding her, his breath fanning over her sweat-dampened skin. She panted as the sensations within her core intensified. Her sex quivered around her fingers. She was close.

Her eyes met his. His gaze was shuttered, but its glow was brilliant and focused solely upon her.

"Come for me, Kiara." His words were clipped, strained, but no less commanding. "Come *with* me."

Removing her slick covered fingers from her channel, she returned them to her clit and circled the tight bud in quick, rough strokes. That was all it took.

"Volcair," she cried as bliss flowered deep inside her, bursting outward until it possessed her. Her toes curled into the bedding, her core spasmed and clenched, and heat swept through her. Breathy moans escaped Kiara, and her eyes begged to close, but she forced them to remain open, to remain locked with Volcair's. Her thighs snapped together, and her pelvis undulated; she needed more. She rubbed harder, faster, prolonging the overwhelming, nearly painful sensations.

"Kiara." Volcair's lips peeled back to once again display his clenched teeth, and he released a sound that was the perfect blend of a pained growl and a pleasured groan. His whole body tensed, toned muscles flexing, as ropes of thick, white seed burst from the head of his cock. They rained on his hand and his sculpted abs. He neither slowed his fist nor broke eye contact with her. If anything, he pumped quicker, more force-fully, his every breath strained and rough.

The sight of him coming undone was titillating and erotic, and she would lock the memory of it away to envision again and again. Volcair was beautiful, especially when his *qal* flared in unrestrained pleasure.

When Kiara could take no more, she stilled her fingers and pressed them firmly against her abused, sensitive clit to soothe it. Her slick covered her inner thighs and had dampened the bed beneath her.

Breath ragged, she relaxed against the pillow. The corners of her mouth quirked up into a smile. Volcair had stilled as well, hand now clamped around the base of his throbbing cock. His lips were parted with his panting breaths, and strands of dark blue hair hung in his face; he looked just a little like he had in the aftermath of their lovemaking back on Janus Six.

Of course, he'd have been quite a bit more disheveled had Kiara been able to have her way with him.

She longed to delve her hands into those blue locks.

"We should do this again," Kiara said, wagging her brows at him.

He laughed, lips lifting into a wide smile. "Absolutely. But next time, I won't just be telling you what I'm going to do, I'm going to ravish every part of you until you're hoarse from screaming my name."

Kiara grinned as a shiver stole through her. She loved this side of him. He'd always been open and honest with her, lowering his guard and showing her parts of him no one else had ever been privy to. But this? This side of him was new and exciting. Though they'd been close as children, they'd spent so many years apart; they had so much to learn and discover from one another—about one another.

And he's once more so far out of my reach.

She tilted her head and sighed, some of her humor fading. She pulled her hand out from between her thighs and rested it on her belly. More than anything, she wanted him here with her, holding her in the wake of what they'd just shared. "I miss you."

"Soon, Kiara. We're almost there. The road has been far too long, but we're finally almost there." With visible reluctance, he finally released his shaft. He spread his fingers and looked down at the seed coating them.

Kiara had the sudden urge to lick his skin clean, and only barely kept her tongue from slipping out. Were he in this room, she'd lick him clean of every drop.

His eyes found hers again, and the look on his face softened as he lowered his hand. "It's late for you, and I'm not far from Arthos. We both need to clean up, and you need sleep."

She stuck her bottom lip out in a pout. "Must you go so soon?"

"Alas, my Juliet, but I must." He smirked, but his eyes remained serious.

Kiara chuckled; even all these years later, she remember those conversations they'd shared while she was away in America. "Our story isn't Romeo and Juliet, remember?"

"It's not. Ours is much, much better. And once I get back to you, there won't be anything in the universe that can separate us again."

She smiled softly. "I love you, Volcair."

"I love you too, my mate." He reached out as though to touch her, and her heart clenched. "I'll call you the moment I'm out of Consortium territory again."

Though she knew these calls would always come to end, she didn't want to say goodbye, didn't want him to go. But very soon, they wouldn't have to.

Patience, Kiara.

Unbidden, a yawn crept up, and she couldn't hold it back.

Volcair smiled. "Sleep, love. Dream of me."

"Always, my star."

ELEVEN

THE SPRAWLING CITYSCAPE of Arthos stretched to the horizon in all directions; there was no question as to why this place had been dubbed the Infinite City, even without taking into account that there were countless layers below the surface that were just as populated and bustling. The architecture and art of a thousand cultures was on display everywhere, all of it interspersed with fountains, waterfalls, pools, and lush vegetation from countless alien worlds. Buildings of every shape and size stood side-by-side across various tiers, interconnected by webs of walkways and terraces that somehow blended flawlessly without looking cluttered.

Pedestrians of more species than Volcair could name filled the streets and walkways, and endless streams of hover vehicles sped through the air in oddly controlled chaos. The motion somehow only complemented the gleaming glass and metal of so many of the buildings.

Volcair studied all this through the side window of the hovercar that had picked him up from the spaceport shuttle station only twenty minutes ago, feeling a contradictory blend of indifference and awe. He'd lived in Arthos for four years during his youth, yearning all along for a view of a far more primitive but more welcoming city—London. Whatever wonders Arthos held, he'd never been taken by them because it was never where he'd wanted to be.

That sentiment was unchanged today, but—like before—he had no choice but to come.

The conversation he'd had with Kiara just before his arrival, however brief, had bolstered his mood. As reluctant as he'd been to end the call, he'd felt good after speaking with her. She'd always been able to cheer him up. Of course, the other surprising but overwhelmingly pleasurable activity in which they'd partaken had helped that mood significantly. He was eager to have her back in his arms again, eager to truly touch her and taste her, to have her in every sense that he could.

But now he was back on Arthos, and he couldn't prevent his spirits from dipping.

He turned his face forward to look out the front window. The Dominion embassy stood ahead, perched on a huge, raised platform that was adorned with carefully cultivated gardens displaying the natural flora of Korous, the volturian homeworld. The building itself was tall and sweeping, with numerous free-floating additions branching off from the top. Each smaller section bore the colors and patterns of an ancestral *qalar* and was joined to the main tower by delicate looking bridges, all of which were arched, enclosed, and run through with those *qal* like designs. All those patterns came together on the central tower, blending into an elegant, flowing combination meant to represent the unity of all the *qalarin*.

Of course, the *qalarin* that had long ago been conquered by the tretin and bred into sedhi—half-volturian, half-tretin beings—were absent. Apparently, Ambassador Syntrell Vantricar Caltraxion had yet to fully succeed in repairing the age-old divide between full blooded volturians and their sedhi cousins.

As the driver neared the embassy, something else caught Volcair's eye. To call it a cluster of buildings would've been a gross understatement; that was how it might've appeared against the backdrop of a wider, seemingly endless city, but the area they covered had to be at least as large as Earth's London. It was the uniformity of those buildings that made them stand out more than anything—they were all dark gray or black, dull but for the violet, red, and yellow lights that were sparsely spread throughout. Most of the buildings were tall and thin, and many had strange, asymmetrical adornments jutting from their sides and tops, some like twisted ladder rungs, most like vicious horns.

That was the closest Consortium sanctum, a space reserved only for the kal'zik, one of the six unfathomably powerful races that had founded and still ruled Arthos.

The kal'zik sanctum was a dark, foreboding place that always seemed under the grip of an oppressive gloom that directly defied the beam of intense quasar light which always kept the surface city brightly lit. It seemed fitting for Volcair to notice it just before visiting his father for the first time in more than five years.

Stop it, Volcair. That mood will only make things worse.

He'd come to Arthos for only one reason, and it hadn't been to brood while taking in the sights. After having to leave Kiara twice, this should've been easy for Volcair. This should've been little more than another brief stop on his journey back to the one place that had always felt like home—Kiara's side. Unfortunately, nothing had ever been simple or easy when it came to Volcair's father.

The driver dropped Volcair near the embassy's front entrance and departed silently. Though he'd just come from Korous, the ancestral homeworld of the volturians and the capital of the Entris Dominion, the nearby plants seemed alien after so many years in space, traveling between unfamiliar worlds. The vegetation made the air fresh and fragrant, but Volcair found himself longing instead for the sweet, earthy smells that surrounded Kiara's childhood home.

He forced himself forward, granting his nerve no time to falter; if he'd faced Kiara after so long, he could face Vantricar.

Volturians of various *qalarin* were all around, along with members of a few different species, all of them walking, talking, or both. No one seemed to pay any attention to Volcair. He found it a welcome change, especially considering how recognizable he'd been as the commander of Janus Six. The anonymity of not wearing a uniform was something he'd forgotten about long ago.

Entering the embassy for the first time in fifteen years was surreal. Part of Volcair felt like a lost, angry sixteen-year-old, bristling with anger he couldn't fully express and having no healthy outlet by which to vent that frustration. He forced those old echoes of emotion aside and instead focused on the embassy's lobby. The furnishings were the same as he remembered—flowing, elegant, and tasteful, the epitome of volturian class and style, featuring intricate, *qal* like glowing patterns to accent it all.

The embassy staff informed him that Vantricar was currently in a meeting and offered to bring him somewhere to wait. To Volcair's surprise, he was led to a familiar set of chambers on one of the upper floors—the very quarters he'd resided in with his father during his four years in Arthos.

Like the embassy's reception area, these rooms seemed unchanged by time. Being here was at once a blessing and a curse; he appreciated the privacy, but the familiarity of the place didn't help him keep those old feelings at bay.

The sitting room was quiet, lit only by a pair of lamps that didn't quite fill the room with their luminescence, and eerily still. It was a place of bitten tongues and held breaths, of unspoken angers and hard, unfocused stares.

No, that's not right. That's just how I used to see it.

There were two matching chairs at the center of the room, angled slightly toward one another. He settled into the one of them and willed his muscles to relax. Even if this place hadn't changed, Volcair had. He wasn't that bitter child anymore.

I suppose I'm a bitter adult instead.

He couldn't deny a hint of truth in the thought, but that only tightened his chest with a pang of sorrow. That's not what he'd ever wanted to be. He'd never imagined that the frustration and hurt could eat him from the inside, could swallow him up, could push him to be so blind, so foolish. And yet here he was.

He tilted his head back, leaning it on the headrest, and closed his eyes. The air in the apartment was a touch cooler than everywhere else, just as his father had always liked it, and it was spiced with a fragrance Volcair hadn't smelled in far too long—*jandori*, flowers from his homeworld that had been his mother's favorite a lifetime ago.

A small smile curled up the corners of Volcair's mouth. Though the memories that smell had once summoned were long since lost to the haziness of passing years, the associated emotions remained. Happiness, playfulness, security, love.

Those had been the foundation of his earliest years. How could he have let himself forget that? How could he not have remembered when Kiara made him feel many of the same things—albeit it with unimagined intensity—during their youth, or while those feelings had grown along with him?

He'd spent fifteen years serving the Entris Dominion. That time had been sparked by his resentment, but only now could he look back and understand his errors. Only now did he truly understand the price of a concept as nebulous as *duty*, though he'd been paying that price since he was a young child.

"I do not think I have ever seen you smile in this place," said Vantricar from the room's entrance. His voice was a little rougher, a little thinner, but unmistakable.

"Perhaps it is best you pretend you did not, Father. I do not wish to taint your memory of my time here."

"You always were sharp with your tongue, my child."

Volcair's smile fell. He opened his eyes and lifted his head.

Ambassador Syntrell Vantricar Caltraxion's shoulders were unbowed by time, but his frame was thinner, and there were fine lines evident around his mouth and on his forehead. His skin was a little paler, a little grayer, and the color of his hair had faded from its old vibrancy. But his *qal* was as clear and bright as ever; Volcair ran his eyes across its visible portions, still able to pick out the pieces that represented his mother's *qal* even after all these years.

"I am sorry, Father. I did not mean for it come across that way."

Vantricar waved a hand dismissively. "You are here, Volcair. I can deal with that tone, so long as you are here."

The pang of sorrow that had seized Volcair's chest a little while ago returned, this time spreading outward in a slow, consuming pulse.

"Come, my son," Vantricar said, "stand up so I may see you."

Volcair pushed himself out of the chair and stepped toward his father. For the first time, he realized that he was taller than Vantricar; his father seemed almost slight now.

Vantricar put his hands on the sides of Volcair's shoulders and smiled at him. "Where is your uniform?"

"My voluntary term ended a month ago, Father."

Now Vantricar's smile drooped, and he knitted his brow. "A month ago? And what of the honors ceremony? Had I known, I would have made arrangements to travel to Korous to attend. I am sure there is still time to do so, though the short notice complicates matters a—"

"The ceremony has already been conducted," Volcair said softly.

Vantricar's expression slackened. For a few moments, he simply stared at Volcair, and then the set of his eyebrows hardened, and his frown deepened. "You did not send word to me? Did not invite me?"

"I was angry at you, Father, and—"

"You were angry at me?" Vantricar's grip on Volcair's shoulders tightened before he dropped his hands. "You have not spoken to me in years, Volcair, and then you purposefully do not invite me to what should have been one of the proudest moments of my life, seeing my son receive full honors from the *qalsarn*? To one of the proudest moments of *your* life?"

"Father—"

"It was enough that I had to learn of your promotion to commander through old acquaintances from home, but this... Volcair..." Vantricar bowed his head and shook it, pressing his lips into a tight line.

The feeling in Volcair's chest only intensified, making it

difficult for him to fill his lungs with much-needed air. His heartbeat thumped in his own ears.

Volcair reached forward and placed his hands on his father's shoulders. "I was foolish, Father. Foolish and petty. Ever since I was small, I carried that anger inside me, and it was so big. I did not know what to do with it, how to bear it. So...I lashed out at you."

Vantricar met Volcair's gaze, features tight. "I lost her too, Volcair." Lifting an arm, Vantricar placed a trembling hand on Volcair's cheek. "You were all I had left after your mother died. You were my only family, my only child. I...I did not know what to do without her. She was my direction, Volcair. All I knew was that I had to cling to you...but that I also had a duty to the Dominion. To our people."

For a moment, Volcair's throat was too constricted to reply. He finally swallowed thickly and ran his tongue across his dry lips. "I know, Father. And I am sorrier than I can say that I did not see your pain through my own."

"I tried to balance my duty to you and my duty to the Dominion. I tried *so*, so hard. I did the best I could, Son. I am sorry it was not enough. I am sorry I failed you." Vantricar dropped his hand from Volcair's face.

"Father..." Volcair searched his father's eyes as though all the right words could be found in them, but he knew that wasn't the case. If the right words existed, they were inside Volcair already, and their foundation lay in what Kiara had told him earlier.

Just be honest with him, Volcair. But be understanding, too.

"If you failed me, Father, then I failed you, as well," he finally said. "Despite my disrespect, you were always patient with me. More patient than I deserved. It has taken so long for me to understand, but I *do* understand now. The service demanded of us from the Dominion...it takes over our lives in so many ways. And I know the thing I was angriest about—when you made me leave Earth—was only you doing as you had to do."

"I had hoped you would move on, Volcair," said Vantricar in a ragged whisper. "I had hoped you would find some semblance of contentment again before you had to serve. I knew you were close to Kiara, but you were all I had. My only reminder of your mother. My only kin. I could not leave you half a universe away... But I fear that the rift I caused between us was at least that large, regardless of my intentions."

Volcair released a heavy breath through his nostrils and squeezed his father's shoulders. "I loved her, Father. I still do. It hurt when you dismissed those feelings. When you disregarded what I knew to be true in my heart. She's made my *qal* glow from the moment I first met her. Having to leave her tore a piece out of me, and then being unable to contact her because of Consortium laws..."

"You were so young, Volcair. I did not think it could be true, especially not of *my* son. You know what our people's stance has always been on such relationships, regardless of how your *qal* reacts."

"I know. And I knew then, too. But that did not change it."

Vantricar frowned. "And I saw the difference in you while you were with her. You were so much brighter. So much happier. I always thought to myself that it is how you might've looked if your mother had survived. If she had been with us."

"We carry Mother in our hearts always," Volcair said, "but she is gone. She has been for so long...and she would not have tolerated the way I behaved because of that loss. She would not have accepted the way I allowed it to fracture our relationship."

"You cannot accept that blame, my son."

"I do accept it, Father." Volcair drew in a deep, steadying breath, lowered his hands, and stepped back, out of Vantricar's reach. What he had to say next could be the turning point of the conversation, of his relationship with his father—but it could turn sharply in either direction. "And though Mother is gone, Kiara is not."

"You mean to go back to her? After all this time?"

Volcair's lips crept up into a small smile. "We found each other. Deep in Dominion space, our paths crossed again after almost twenty years. In the vastness of the universe, what could that meeting have been other than fate?"

"I sense there is a story to be told."

Volcair nodded. "There is, but only one thing is important, Father—I will be returning to Earth soon, and Kiara and I will be wed."

Vantricar's brows rose, his eyes rounded, and his lips parted.

"I understand the expectations, Father. I understand the way our people view it. I understand that it may even tarnish your reputation. But you must understand that it is my destiny, and it always has been. I love her, and we are mates. Those truths are indisputable.

"Whether I receive your approval or not, I will follow through with this. But it would mean everything to me, Father, if you attended this ceremony. It is the only ceremony that matters to *me*."

Vantricar released a soft huff of air, dropped his gaze to the floor, and shook his head. "There are those within the Dominion government who will frown upon this—perhaps more of them than I can guess. They may use it against me as leverage, threaten to expose me as not being here in service to our people. But I do not care." He met Volcair's gaze again. His features were hard now, they were determined. "I have spent decades fulfilling my duty to the Entris Dominion, and if those years of service do not speak for themselves, what comes after does not matter."

Vantricar stepped closer and placed his hands on Volcair's shoulders again. "Volcair, my son, I can think of no honor greater than witnessing the joining of you and your mate. And I will do everything in my power to ensure that union is acknowledged as valid by the Dominion whether they like it or not."

Before Volcair could respond, Vantricar drew him into a tight hug. It was so unexpected that Volcair didn't know how to react for a second or two; volturians, especially dignified, ranking volturians, didn't hug. But the warmth, affection, and desperation in the gesture were so powerful that he found himself returning the embrace.

So simple a gesture couldn't make up for decades of conflict between them...but it was more than enough to speed the process of healing from that strife. For the first time in so long, Volcair felt like he truly had a father.

He only wished that he'd realized his own errors—his own stubbornness, his own pettiness—a long time ago.

"Thank you, Volcair," Vantricar finally said when he pulled back. "Thank you for inviting me. For coming to see me."

"Thank you, Father, for all you've done for me—especially the things I could not appreciate when I was younger."

"I suppose the Dominion will now view my push to sponsor a Consortium invitation to the terrans as biased," Vantricar said with a chuckle.

Volcair tilted his head, brow furrowing. "You have been working to have the terrans invited to Arthos?"

"Since the day I took this post, my son. It may not have seemed so to you back then, but I very much enjoyed our time on Earth. Isaiah Moore and his wife, Jada, were amongst my dearest friends. But these matters are deeply political in nature, and the Dominion has been hesitant to sponsor the terrans despite the deep alliance we have formed with them."

For a few seconds, Volcair could only stare at his father. When he attempted to speak, a small, disbelieving chuckle emerged from his throat first. "You have been working toward that for all these years?"

"I have."

"Father, I... Again, I am sorry."

"As am I, Volcair."

"It is... It is more important now than ever that the terrans are invited to Arthos. That will afford them more of the protections they need."

Now Vantricar's brows knitted. "What do you mean?"

"My encounter with Kiara occurred because her ship had been hijacked by pirates who intended to sell her and her crew into slavery. We have been seeing a trend amongst those slavers—terrans are considered exotic, and they are increasingly in demand on those markets. Without access to the alliances and resources available on Arthos, I fear they will remain unable to counter such efforts."

Vantricar's expression hardened with a passion and dedication Volcair had rarely seen from him. "All the more reason for me to press our allies—especially those who joined us on Earth those years ago—to cosponsor the application. I promise you, Son, that I will see this done as quickly as possible. What of Kiara? Is she all right?"

"Fortunately, neither she nor her crew came to any lasting harm. She made it home safely today."

"Good. She was always such a bright, lively girl. The universe would have been darker for lack of her."

Volcair couldn't help but see that as a massive understatement, but he understood that his opinion might've been considered biased.

"Father, if you have time..." Volcair gestured to the chairs. "It has been a long while. We both must have so much to tell."

Vantricar smiled, raised his left wrist, and activated his holocom. He flicked through a few options on the projection screen. "My afternoon is suddenly free, my son. Are you ready for something to drink now?"

TWELVE

London, Capital of the United Terran Federation, Earth
  Terran Year 2101

KIARA COULD HARDLY CONTAIN her excitement as she stood in the dressing room with her mother, who was applying the finishing touches to Kiara's hair. The normally unruly curls were pulled back, twisted, and pinned in place, adorned with little white flowers.

"Stop fidgeting," Jada scolded around the decorative pin in her mouth. She plucked the pin out and inserted it into Kiara's hair.

"I can't! He's here, Mum. It's been weeks since I last saw him."

Jada moved to stand in front of Kiara and smiled. Though the woman was in her sixties, she was as beautiful as ever. Her eyes were watery with tears as she pressed her palm to her daughter's cheek. "You make a gorgeous bride, Kiara. Look."

Kiara turned toward the large wall-mounted mirror. Her

gown was a mix of human and volturian fashions—a flowing skirt with slits along the sides to reveal her legs and a sleeveless, corseted top that left her arms and shoulders bare. Rather than the traditional white, the fabric was the same color as Volcair's *qal*—the same markings that were now permanently inked on Kiara's skin.

It was her gift to Volcair.

The practice was custom among the volturians, and she wanted to give him that part of his culture. She wanted everyone to look upon her and know, without a doubt, whose mate she was.

The surprise was the reason she hadn't let Volcair see her—even during their calls—since he'd returned to Earth a few days earlier. Though it had driven her crazy to stay away from him, she knew it'd be worth the look in his eyes when he finally saw her.

The door slid open, and Kiara turned to see her father enter the room. She beamed at him.

"Ah, my little girl," Isaiah said, opening his arms to her.

Kiara embraced him, and he squeezed her tight. "Hi, Daddy."

"It feels as though you were sitting on my knee only yesterday. Where have all the years gone?" He drew back, taking gentle hold of her arms. "Let me look at you."

She smiled up at her father.

His eyes were alight with pride. "You are beautiful, Kiara."

"Thanks, Daddy."

"Oh! Volcair asked me to give you something." Isaiah dipped his hand into his pocket and withdrew a small, square silver box. He handed it to her.

Without hesitation, Kiara opened it. Her heart overflowed with love for Volcair as she removed her balus stone pendant from the box. The chain, which had been broken by the tretin pirate, had been replaced. It looked to be a mix of white gold and tristeel now, just as beautiful as before but far stronger—just like her connection with Volcair. "My necklace!"

She'd been distraught when she left Janus Six, convinced she'd lost the necklace. She'd torn the room apart, desperate to find it, but it had seemingly vanished. Volcair had vowed to find it. Had it been in his possession all along?

Whether or not it was, he fixed *it.*

"Help me put it on, Mum?"

"Of course," Jada said.

Kiara looked at her father as Jada slipped the necklace around Kiara's neck and clasped the chain. Once it was in place, the balus stone hung just below her collarbone.

Isaiah reached out and took Kiara's hand in both of his. The joy in his eyes dimmed slightly. "I can't tell you how sorry I am for all the years you lost because of my silence."

"Don't." Kiara leaned forward and pressed a kiss on her father's cheek. "I know why you did it, Daddy, and I don't blame you."

Had he understood the truth, he never would've kept the secret from her. She wasn't angry with him; she knew he'd acted out of love and concern.

"It's in the past," she said softly, drawing back to smile at her father. "We won't look back. Only forward."

Isaiah smiled in return, his eyes misting. "My wise, beautiful girl." He looped his arm around hers. "Are you ready to marry your mate?"

Kiara's heart thundered. "I've been ready my whole life."

VOLCAIR GLANCED toward the entryway at the end of the long aisle for what must've been the thousandth time. The months had gone by with surprising speed, but this waiting—waiting for his bride, who he had not seen in person since her time on Janus Six—felt eternal. His heart pounded, not due to nervousness, but anticipation. Cypher sat on the floor beside him, tail swishing seemingly in time with Volcair's heartbeat, restless and eager.

Kiara and Volcair had spoken through voice communication for hours and hours since his arrival on Earth several days before, but she hadn't allowed him so much as a glimpse of her. Though he'd heard the longing in her voice, she'd refused to meet him, refused to invite him to her house.

She'd said the extra wait would make it more special when they finally saw each other.

His eyes shifted from the empty entryway to the people seated on either side of the aisle—terrans on the same side as Volcair was standing, volturians on the side Kiara would stand. It was an old Volturian tradition for such ceremonies, made more meaningful when the mates' *qalarin*—or in this case, species—were different. It was a sign that the families supported the union.

Vantricar had come, along with several other high-ranking Dominion officials and ambassadors. Volcair only cared about his father's presence, but it was heartening to see those other guests—it meant his union to Kiara would be recognized both by the United Terran Federation and the Entris Dominion. He knew it didn't mean the Dominion itself was wildly altering its stance on interspecies relationships, but this was a start.

Of course, he'd have followed through whether they'd approved or not. His service to the Dominion was over; he'd more than earned the right to live without their contempt for following his heart.

Kiara was all that mattered to him.

A sudden swell of music hushed the crowd's quiet conversations and drew Volcair out of his thoughts. When he looked to the entryway again, it was no longer empty.

Isaiah and Jada stood in the opening, positioned to either side of their daughter. Volcair's eyes fell on Kiara, and his breath caught in his throat.

She was radiant, more beautiful than ever before, and her smile—a smile just for him—filled the room with light and joy. The white-blue of her dress contrasted her dark skin while perfectly complementing the markings on her face, neck, and shoulders—markings that matched his *qal* exactly.

Volcair's chest swelled with pride, and that old, familiar warmth—the warmth he'd first felt when he met a little terran girl so many years ago—spread outward from his heart. He hadn't fully understood as a child why his parents had taken on one another's *qal*, but he did now. He'd not expected Kiara to take his and would never have asked it of her, but that she'd done so was a sign of devotion and love he feared he could never match.

He clasped his hands together at his front and squeezed them; it was all he could do to keep himself from going to Kiara as her parents slowly escorted her down the aisle. He couldn't take his eyes off her; she was more than he deserved, more than he could ever earn, but she was still *his*.

When the trio reached the bottom of the low steps leading to the dais upon which Volcair stood, Jada and Isaiah each kissed Kiara on the cheek and stepped away.

Kiara tilted her head back to face him, locking her eyes with his as she climbed the dais. Her smile widened with each step.

Unable to restrain himself any longer, Volcair descended to meet her, holding out his hands. She took them, and fire flared along his *qal*. Its light, more intense than ever, bathed Kiara and set the markings on her skin aglow.

His heated blood rushed to his loins, and he clenched his teeth at a sudden, powerful surge of arousal. He'd only known her touch—her *true*, intimate touch—for the handful of days she'd spent with him on Janus Six. It had not been nearly enough. He needed to have her *now*.

"What do you think?" she whispered.

Volcair released one of her hands to brush his fingertips over the *qal* on her cheek. "I think you outshine the stars."

Her eyes softened, and an instant later, she pressed her lips against his. He slid his hand into her hair and deepened the kiss, hungry for a taste of her, hungry for so much more. He barely held in the groan that threatened to rise from his chest. Only the presence of the crowd kept him from laying her upon the dais and having her then and there—and only because she was for his eyes alone.

She slowly drew away, catching her lower lip between her teeth. "I know we're supposed to kiss after, but I just couldn't wait."

The officiant cleared his throat.

Both Volcair and Kiara turned their heads toward him. The human was grinning despite his obvious effort to contain his mirth.

"It is joyous to see two people in love," he said before gesturing to the top of the dais. "Shall we proceed?"

Volcair led Kiara to stand before the officiant. They stopped and faced one another, joining hands in the space between their bodies. She trembled lightly, but there was only love and anticipation in her eyes. His heart quickened.

For years he'd thought he'd lost her, for years he'd been consumed by bitterness and loneliness, until his Kiara, his shining star, reappeared in his life. She stood before him now, a dazzling manifestation of all his dreams and desires in the flesh. She was his everything.

She was his fate.

AUTHOR'S NOTE

We hope you all enjoyed Volcair and Kiara's story! We had so much fun writing this, and had just as much fun when we were able to expand it from its original restricted word count in the *Pets in Space*® *Anthology* to make it 50% longer.

If you are just beginning your journey through our Infinite City series, we hope you enjoy it! This was simply a prequel, and Silent Lucidity will take you into deep into the Infinite City itself.

If you have a spare moment, we'd love it if you could leave a review for *Entwined Fates*. Thank you again for reading and for all your support!

And if you're on Facebook, come join our private reader group! We'd love to see you there. We share all kinds of news and art.

The Weaver

The Delver

The Hunter

<u>THE CURSED ONES</u>

<u>His Darkest Craving</u>

His Darkest Desire

<u>ALIENS AMONG US</u>

<u>Taken by the Alien Next Door</u>

<u>Stalked by the Alien Assassin</u>

<u>Claimed by the Alien Bodyguard</u>

Saved by the Alien Crime Boss

<u>STANDALONE TITLES</u>

<u>Claimed by an Alien Warrior</u>

<u>Dustwalker</u>

<u>Escaping Wonderland</u>

<u>Yearning For Her</u>

<u>The Warlock's Kiss</u>

<u>Ice Bound: Short Story</u>

<u>ISLE OF THE FORGOTTEN</u>

<u>Make Me Burn</u>

<u>Make Me Hunger</u>

<u>Make Me Whole</u>

<u>Make Me Yours</u>

<u>VALOS OF SONHADRA COLLABORATION</u>

<u>Tiffany Roberts - Undying</u>

<u>Tiffany Roberts - Unleashed</u>

<u>VENYS NEEDS MEN COLLABORATION</u>

<u>Tiffany Roberts - To Tame a Dragon</u>

<u>Tiffany Roberts – To Love a Dragon</u>

ABOUT THE AUTHOR

Tiffany Roberts is the pseudonym for Tiffany and Robert Freund, a husband and wife writing duo. The two have always shared a passion for reading and writing, and it was their dream to combine their mighty powers to create the sorts of books they want to read. They write character driven sci-fi and fantasy romance, creating happily-ever-afters for the alien and unknown.

Sign up for our Newsletter!
Check out our social media sites and more!
http://www.authortiffanyroberts.com